FRIGHT WATCH

The COLLECTORS

FRIGHT WATCH
The COLLECTORS

LORIEN LAWRENCE

Amulet Books

New York

Cataloging-in-Publication Data has been applied for
and may be obtained from the Library of Congress.

ISBN 978-1-4197-5604-7

Text copyright © 2021 Lorien Lawrence
Illustrations by Gilles Ketting
Title lettering by David Coulson
Book design by Jade Rector

Published in 2021 by Amulet Books, an imprint of ABRAMS.

Printed and bound in U.S.A.
10 9 8 7 6 5 4 3 2 1

Amulet Books are available at special discounts when purchased in quantity for premiums and promotions as well as fundraising or educational use. Special editions can also be created to specification. For details, contact specialsales@abramsbooks.com or the address below.

ABRAMS The Art of Books
195 Broadway, New York, NY 10007
abramsbooks.com

For Ruby and Leo

CHAPTER 1

It's strange being on Goodie Lane without seeing the Oldies. Their houses look different with their colors stripped away, and most of the rosebushes died along with their original owners: Bea, Attwood, the Browns, and the Smiths. Instead, five new neighbors have taken their places: young women who, from across the street, all look like they might be in their mid- to late twenties. Mike and I nicknamed them the Ladies in White because they're always dressed in shades of ivory and bone. We haven't officially met them—not yet, anyway. But from a distance, they seem pretty normal, which should be a welcome change to Goodie Lane.

But sometimes—just sometimes—when they wave hello, a coldness seeps through my skin, and I can't help but shiver despite the mild September warmth.

"Sup, Parker." Mike startles me as he joins me on the sidewalk. He smirks and lowers his Yankees hat over his eyes.

I nudge him playfully in the arm. "Are you *ever* going to be on time?"

He pretends to think it over before shrugging. "I need my beauty sleep."

"Come on," I moan, tugging him forward. "We can't be late for our first day of school."

"These legs are never late," he says, doing a little two-step that makes both of us laugh.

We start off down Goodie Lane. Before we turn the corner onto Main Street, I wave a quick goodbye to Billy, who watches us pathetically from the living room window. He always has a hard time being left alone when I go back to school. He lives for summer days, going on sunny walks with Mike and me. *See you soon, boy.* I make a mental note to give him extra hugs when I get home.

"So what's your schedule like?" Mike asks. We've fallen into step with each other on the main road, our shoulders touching as we move. He holds out his hand. "Let me see if we have any classes together."

I dig in my pocket and take out my phone, pulling up my schedule. Mike takes it and squints at the screen.

"Oh, you're so lucky, Parker."

I take back my phone and eye him. "Why am I lucky?"

"Because you're going to get to be lab partners with this genius." He pats himself on the chest.

"Like I even need your help in science. I got an A last year all on my own, thank you very much." I flip my ponytail. "Besides, what makes you think I want to be your lab partner?" I try to throw him a sassy look, but I can't keep a straight face, and Mike can see right through my bluff.

"Whatever, Parker. You know we make the best team."

I feel a smile bloom. "You're right," I admit. "We kind of do."

We spend the rest of the walk kicking a stone back and forth on the sidewalk, talking about which teachers we heard were cool, and which ones we wish we could swap. Mike shares his granola bar with me and then throws the wrapper into the trash bin outside the school's entrance.

"Buckets," he praises himself as the wrapper swooshes in.

I ignore him, turning instead to the Rocky Hill Middle School sign.

"You ready for another year?" Mike asks, following my gaze.

"After this summer, I'm ready for anything," I tell him.

"*Quinnie!*"

I spin around at the sound of my best friend's voice. Zoe skates toward us, her backpack bouncing behind her as she rolls. She hops off her board and throws her arms around me as though we hadn't just hung out yesterday.

"Hey, Mike," she says, pulling away.

He nods at her. "Sup, Zoe."

"I don't feel like an eighth grader," she says, peering warily at the building. She then picks up her board, hugging it against her hip. "Aren't we supposed to feel different? Older or something?" She sets her green eyes on me. "Do *you* feel any different, Quinn?"

I shrug and look away. "Nope, I feel exactly the same as I did last year." A statement that couldn't be further from the truth, given what I went through this summer with the Oldies. But unlike my best friend, I'm actually kind of looking forward to being back at school. School has a routine. It's normal. It's safe.

"Let's just get this over with," she mumbles. "Come on."

With this, she leads Mike and me through the double doors. Side by side, we enter the crowded hallways, bumping against students we haven't seen in two months, their smiles genuine with the excitement of a new year and a fresh start. We barely get two feet deep before Lex and Kaylee ambush us.

"I can't believe we're eighth graders!" Lex squeals, bouncing up and down. "Can you believe it? I can't believe it."

Zoe raises a steady eyebrow. "Calm down. It's just *school.*" She makes a face as if the word leaves a bad taste in her mouth.

Lex smiles. "But school has *people*. Mom says I'm an extrovert, so I need to be surrounded by people."

"Weren't you the one who was *so* excited for summer vacation?" Kaylee asks, her eyes twinkling behind her glasses.

Lex sighs. "Yeah, but then I got bored. There's nothing to do in South Haven! I swear, I'm going to go to college far away from here. Like San Francisco. Or New York City. Or at least out of Connecticut."

"You kind of have to get through eighth grade first," I point out, stifling a laugh.

"And high school," Kaylee adds.

Lex dismisses us with a wave of her hand. "Minor details." Her brown eyes flicker to Mike, seeming to just notice him. "Oh, hey."

"Hey, Lex," he says, smiling his easy smile.

I suddenly feel the weight of my friends' eyes on Mike and me, breathing in our every move. As far as they know, Mike and I are still dating. Last spring, we started a whole fake romance thing as a way of explaining why we were spending so much time together during the Oldies investigation. It worked—they totally bought it. Originally the plan was to "break up" after we got rid of our neighbors, but that was months ago, and neither of us has made any move to end it. Sometimes I feel guilty about lying, but other times I'm secretly grateful to have something still connecting me to Mike.

"You guys have a good summer?" he asks, addressing my friends as he pulls his hat farther down.

"It was OK," Zoe answers for everyone. "How was yours?"

Mike shrugs. "Pretty boring. Especially July."

We both laugh at this, and my friends give us a strange look, oblivious to our inside joke. They don't know a thing about the Oldies. To the rest of South Haven, Ms. Bea and her crew were just a group of generous senior citizens who splashed money around town and looked good for their ages. Rumor has it that they all retired to Florida. Only Mike, Grandma Jane, Red, and I know the truth. I heard that Philippa Dash wanted to write an article for the school paper about the Oldies' sudden move, but her cousin and editor, Tyler Dash, told her that nobody would read it, so instead they're planning a different feature for the first issue of the *Rocky Hill News*. Honestly, I'm kind of relieved: the sooner that South Haven forgets about the Oldies, the better.

"Umm . . ." Zoe says, looking back and forth between Mike and me. "Did we miss something? Do you need a minute? Because we can leave."

I hadn't realized that I was staring at Mike. I blink and quickly clear my throat. "No, it's cool," I tell Zoe. Then I throw one last glance at my fake boyfriend. "I'll see you around."

"Later, Parker." With this, Mike walks away, joining his own friends by his locker.

Zoe grins at me. "That was . . ."

"Don't start," I warn her.

Lex grabs my sleeve. "Hey, where did you get that shirt? It's so cute," she says, thankfully changing the subject.

"You were with me when I bought it," I tell her. "You picked it out for me."

"Oh yeah! I have good taste." She furrows her eyebrows. "But why didn't you wear the one I bought you for your birthday? Don't you like it?"

"No, I love it. I'll wear it soon, I promise."

The first bell rings, startling everyone in the hallway.

"Who do you guys have for homeroom?" I ask, pulling out my schedule.

"Mrs. Pugliese," Zoe says. "You?"

"Mr. Feagin again."

"Me too," Lex says. "Kaylee, you're with Zoe, right?" She waits for Kaylee to nod before tugging me down the hall.

"See you at lunch!" I call over my shoulder.

As we walk, Lex gushes on and on about all of her new back-to-school clothes, and how the woman at the salon apparently "messed up" her pixie cut, even though to me, it looks just as awesome as ever. She talks loud and fast, and there's no room for me to add anything other than a few cools and yeses. Some people get annoyed with Lex, complaining that she's too extra, but I've grown to love her tangents. She's what Mom would call a "free spirit"—kind of like my grandma Jane, but way more stylish.

Lex finally takes a break as Mr. Feagin goes through the attendance.

"Do you have track practice today?" she asks after Mr. Feagin sits back down.

I shake my head. "Nope. Tomorrow is the first one."

"You're the captain this year, right?"

"Me and Jess are co-captains." I secretly love the way that the word *captain* feels against my tongue.

Lex high-fives me. "Nice. What about Kaylee?"

"Not this year."

"And Mike? Is he the boys' captain now that Ramon is in high school?" Before I can tell her Shreyas is actually captain this year, Lex smiles. "Aww, you're blushing! You're thinking about him, aren't you?" She pokes me in the arm. "Aren't you?" She shrugs when I don't immediately respond. "It's cool. You don't have to be embarrassed, Quinn. I think you guys are cute together. I mean, the way he *looks* at you."

"How does he look at me?" I ask despite myself.

She forms a heart shape with her hands.

My skin grows hot just as the bell rings.

"See you at lunch," I tell her, before we scurry off in opposite directions.

The rest of the day is uneventful. Class after class is the same old first-day-of-school stuff: teachers going through classroom expectations and handing out papers that they know half of the students are just going to lose. When the final bell rings, I make a beeline for my locker.

"Ready?" Zoe asks, holding her skateboard under her arm.

I swing my backpack over my shoulders. "Yeah."

"You have your skateboard?"

"Nope. I walked to school with Mike."

She sighs. "Guess I'll carry mine. Let's go."

We walk outside, where we weave around potholes and stray sticks from last night's storm. There's an energy on the streets: kids running off buses, grabbing their bikes, chasing and hollering at one another as if the heat of summer wasn't already over. We pass by Frank's Quick Stop and see a few kids from school drinking sodas on the stoop. It isn't long before we reach the gazebo and the town center, along with the plaza of old-fashioned brick buildings housing Cucina Della Nonna, the pharmacy, the hardware store, and our favorite after-school hangout, Harvey's.

The cold, sweet air makes me smile every time I enter the lime green and pale pink shop. Servers—mostly local high schoolers—roll around on skates, delivering milk-shakes that are piled high with homemade whipped cream and ruby-colored cherries. I take a deep breath in and look around. Kaylee and Lex wave to us from a corner booth.

"Over here!"

Zoe and I make our way over and fall against the pastel cushions, tucking our bags and Zoe's skateboard beneath our feet.

"How'd you get here so fast?" I ask.

"My mom drove us," Kaylee says. "We both have study hall last period on Thursdays."

"Lucky," Zoe moans.

"Very lucky," Lex agrees. "And we already ordered for you guys. We're trying the back-to-school special. It has Milky Ways blended in. I don't know what that has to do with school, but it sounds *amazing*."

"Cool," Zoe and I say, closing our menus.

I look at Kaylee across the table. "This is way better than practice."

"Definitely!" She beams, then suddenly makes her face all business again. "But tomorrow we'll make up for it. I saw Jess on the way out, and she said she already has a list of new drills that she wants to ask Coach to try—"

Lex clears her throat loudly. "Nope, not having it."

Kaylee blinks. "Not having what?"

Lex waves her hands. "*This*. Track talk. School talk. None of it." She slams her palms against the table for emphasis.

"Well, what do *you* want to talk about?" I ask.

Before Lex can answer, a server skates on over, balancing a tray of chocolaty-caramelly-looking goodness hiding beneath a mountain of whipped cream.

"Back-to-school specials all around," she says. "Who gets the one with the rainbow sprinkles?"

"She does," Lex says, nodding to me. "We know you love them," she adds, smiling.

I thank her and pull the shake toward me, taking a divine sip. This drink is everything good in the world, the perfect balance of salt and sweet. The four of us thank the server and immediately begin slurping until our brains freeze, at which point we count to five as we press our tongues against the roofs of our mouths, trying not to laugh.

"Pretty soon it's going to be too cold for milkshakes," Kaylee points out.

"Don't say that," Zoe moans. "I live for this place. Besides, school literally just started."

"Nope, Kay's right," Lex says. "We need to start thinking about our group Halloween costumes."

"It's too early for that," Zoe says, waving her off.

"It's never too early," Lex insists. "Especially if we want to get Marion to do our makeup."

Marion Jones is Rocky Hill's resident makeup artist. Even though she's only in eighth grade, she can do it all— from beauty to monster to everything in between. Kids have to get on a waiting list for her to do their costume makeup, and the closer it gets to Halloween, the harder she is to book.

Lex points her straw at Zoe. "And you *are* being part of the group this year. I want one cohesive look. Something stylish and scary."

"I was thinking of going as a tub of cheese puffs," Zoe says. She blinks at Lex's horrified expression. "What? It'd be funny."

Kaylee and I giggle.

"It would be kind of funny," I admit.

Lex shakes her head. "You're all impossible."

We settle back and drink our shakes. Kaylee is the first to finish hers, slurping loudly as the straw hits the bottom of the glass. I scoop up a chunk of Milky Way with my spoon.

"Good choice on the milkshakes," I tell Lex.

She doesn't seem to hear me. Instead, she has a dreamy look in her eyes. "I wonder if anything interesting will happen this year," she says.

"Like what?" Zoe asks. "Redecorating your room *again*?"

Lex bites her bottom lip. "No—Mom says I'm cut off. She wouldn't have time to help me anyway. She's so preoccupied with the twins."

Kaylee chews on her straw. "Are they trying out for the winter play?"

Lex's older brothers, Carlos and Julian, are kind of a big deal in the South Haven theater world. They've been in every play and musical since the sixth grade. Mrs. Vega has spent years driving them between voice lessons, dance lessons, and auditions. I saw them on stage during the high school's spring performance, and they *are* really good.

"I don't know. Probably," Lex sighs. "I just feel like this town is so basic, you know? Nothing ever happens here."

"Be careful what you wish for," I say under my breath.

"I'm serious," she whines. "I want an adventure for once."

I stiffen at her words, knowing all too well how overrated adventures can be. We sit in silence for a moment that feels too long. Zoe finally ends the subject by letting out a small belch. I hit her with my menu. The four of us laugh and finish our shakes, before scraping together our allowance money to pay the bill. Then we stumble out onto the sidewalk, squinting against the sun.

"Want to hang out at my house?" I suggest.

"Good idea," Zoe says, dropping her board with a thud. "You live the closest."

I lead the way as we bob around quaint side streets, past mismatched homes and loose cats, and a little league game where half of the home team seems to be crying. Within minutes, we reach the pond near Goodie Lane: this is the same pond that gave the Oldies their energy, the same one that claimed Mary Hove's life back in the sixties. I very nearly ended up just like Mary Hove—drowned by a vengeful ghost witch—but Mike pulled me out of the pond scum just in time. Even though I know that the Oldies are dead, I still feel the familiar tingling sensation in my hands whenever I'm near these waters.

"Hurry up, Quinn," Zoe says, tugging me around the embankment toward my cul-de-sac.

Once we've pushed past the low-hanging trees, we land on Goodie Lane. Zoe starts to skate in lazy circles around the rest of us as we walk in a line.

"Hey," Kaylee suddenly says. "How are the new neighbors?" She nods over to a woman across the street, just coming out of her house. She looks about as old as my fifth-grade social studies teacher, Ms. Charles, who once told us she was twenty-six. But my neighbor is much more fashionable than Ms. Charles, from her white-blonde hair falling in neat waves down her back, to her simple gold necklace, to her silk shift dress, which catches the sun in a way that makes her look ethereal.

"You mean the Ladies in White?" I shrug. "I don't know. They don't talk much."

"They seem way cooler than your old neighbors," Lex breathes.

Zoe snorts beside me. "Yeah, but at least they wore some color. I mean, say what you want about Ms. Bea, but she had pizzazz."

"White is chic," Lex argues.

"But even the *sign* is white—look."

Our four heads turn toward the direction of Zoe's pointed

finger. One of the Ladies in White is directing a thick man holding a hammer; she smiles at him and gestures toward the sign lying on the grass.

"What's the sign say?" Kaylee asks, squinting.

"I can't tell."

"Shh. He's putting it up. Look."

Together, we stand and watch the man twitch his mustache as my neighbor tells him exactly where to place the sign. He nods and smiles, his eyes not moving from her face until she gives him a nod, and he swings his hammer and fixes the signpost into the ground.

I read the board out loud: *"Design on Goodie."* I frown. "Design *what* on Goodie?"

Lex squeals beside me. "Don't you get it?"

"No," Zoe says. "We don't."

Lex rolls her eyes. *"Design.* Like interior design."

"Oh, like decorating?" Kaylee asks. "My mom loves decorating. For Christmas each year, we go all out with lights and—"

"No, no, no," Lex says, shaking her head. "Designing is totally different than decorating!"

"How?" Zoe asks.

Lex sighs. "It just *is.*"

The mustached man then attaches a smaller sign below the first on two silver hooks: **OPEN HOUSE ON SUNDAY 6–8.**

"What's an open house?" Zoe asks, squinting at the addition.

"It's like a party," Lex says. "You know, like a way for them to introduce themselves to the neighborhood." She turns to us. "We *have* to go."

"Speak for yourself," Zoe mumbles. "I'm not going to some boring decorator's party."

"Interior. *Design!*"

"Whatever."

We continue to watch as my neighbor shakes the man's hand.

"I'd die for that dress," Lex breathes.

Suddenly the Lady in White turns and sets her gray eyes on Lex in a way that feels deliberate. There was no chance she could have heard Lex from so far away. I feel goosebumps prickle along my skin as Lex stares back at her, their eyes locked, which makes us all stop. No one says a word. No one moves. It's like we're frozen.

Only after the Lady in White turns away and saunters back over to her house are we able to move again.

Zoe blinks. "Am I the only one who thought that was weird?"

"Very weird," I say, my arms tingling from the cold.

Kaylee turns toward Lex. "She was staring at you pretty hard. Do you know her?"

Lex's eyes are still focused across the street, on the

DESIGN ON GOODIE sign now standing tall in the Lady in White's front yard. "Not yet," she says under her breath.

I shake my head and tug on her arm. "Come on," I urge, suddenly anxious to get inside. I lead the four of us up my front steps, throwing one last look across the street. The woman is still hovering on her landing, watching us. I quickly close the door behind us.

CHAPTER 2

I don't give the Lady in White another thought until the next morning, when my phone wakes me up with the *Batman* theme song. Mike's insisted on making it my ringtone when he calls, even though he knows how annoying it is.

"What's wrong?" I ask in lieu of a *hello*. "Are you bailing on our run?" I glance at the clock: it's 6:05, way too early for our normal 6:30 start time.

"Look out your window," he mumbles.

I slide off my bed, half-expecting rain or hail or something weather-related. I gasp when I peer through the glass. "You're already out there?"

"Yup. Just waiting on you, lazybones."

"OK, I'll be down in five minutes," I tell him, before hanging up and rushing over to my closet.

I'm dressed and downstairs in four, giving Billy a quick

pat on the head before making my way out the door. Mike's warming up in the driveway.

"Come on, you're burning daylight," he says with a smirk.

I eye him suspiciously. Mike's not a morning person. "What's gotten into you?"

"Nothing. Just couldn't sleep. Are we talking or are we running?" Then, without waiting for an answer, he takes off down Goodie Lane.

"Hey!" I cry, trotting to catch up.

Automatically, my neck cranes toward the white houses across the street: they're quiet and dark, as if everyone inside is still sleeping. I know it's been months, but it's still strange not seeing the Oldies out there with their roses and their teacups each morning. I know I should feel grateful, but for some reason, I don't.

"Come on!" Mike calls, waiting at the edge of the cul-de-sac.

I throw one last look over my shoulder before taking off after him, and together we disappear through the woods.

Mike jerks his head toward me, smirking at me in the dull light. "That all you got, Parker?"

I bolt forward, catching up.

This is what freedom feels like. This is the reason I continue to run morning after morning. It's the only part of the day when my body doesn't feel on edge. It's like my limbs can finally catch up to my heartbeat, which in all honesty hasn't felt the same since last Fourth of July, when I stood on this same pavement and watched the Oldies burn, their stolen bodies twisting and bursting at the seams before turning to ash at my feet. On nights when it's extra hot outside, I can still hear them screaming. Even when I'm just walking by here, I can't help but feel like my senses are on high alert.

I guess that's the thing about thwarting the plot of an evil witch—you never really relax afterward.

So you run.

When I get home, Billy's still sprawled out on his dog bed, looking half-asleep. I bustle around him, gathering my things for school.

"I'll see you later, boy," I tell him, patting his head. Then I shout a quick goodbye to Mom, who's getting ready upstairs.

"Bye, honey," she calls back. "Love you!"

"Love you, too."

And with this, I'm out the door with my backpack slung over my shoulder. Once again, Mike is already waiting in my driveway. He tuts at me.

"Late again, Parker. That's two for two."

"You're just early," I tell him.

He tugs down the brim of his hat. "If you say so."

We start down Goodie Lane, when suddenly all four doors swing open across the street at exactly the same time, as if they're on some kind of weird timer. Mike and I freeze in place and watch our beautiful neighbors descend their porch steps as if they're floating. Two of them emerge from the same house. In an instant, all five of them are standing in front of us, smiling. Bea's replacement gazes down at me, and I'm reminded of yesterday with Lex, of the way the woman's gray eyes locked onto my friend's, freezing her.

"Good morning," the woman says, her voice as smooth as honey. "I've been meaning to introduce myself. My name is Abigail." She doesn't reach out to shake hands the way my mom or Grandma Jane would; instead, she keeps her palms pressed against her sides.

Up close, she's even more beautiful, and it takes Mike and me a moment to answer.

"H-*hi*," I stutter. "I'm Quinn." I look at Mike, who is standing beside me with his mouth hanging open. I whack him in the arm.

"Mike," he blurts. "I'm Mike."

Abigail nods at us politely. Then, with a quick flick of the wrist, she signals to the other Ladies in White, who step forward and introduce themselves one by one.

"I'm Jade," the first woman says, arching a brow and tilting her head to one side. Her large, gold hoop earrings catch the sun and reflect into my eyes, blinding me for a second.

She seems to notice and gives a little laugh before tilting her head the other way. She's got russet-brown skin, and her hair is bleached blonde and cropped short, exposing her ears and her long, slender neck. Like Abigail, she doesn't extend a hand for us to shake; instead, she links arms with the woman standing next to her—the one who came out of the same house as Jade.

"And this is Eleanor," she tells us.

Eleanor smiles but doesn't address Mike or me directly. She has pale pink skin and straight, honey-blonde hair that's parted down the middle, framing her face like curtains. Both she and Jade are wearing minidresses with bell sleeves. Their brown and black boots are the only hint of color in otherwise white outfits. They stand very close together—closer than the other women. Eleanor leans over and whispers something in Jade's ear, which makes Jade laugh, tilting her pretty head back.

I shift, wondering what—or who—the joke is about.

The next woman steps forward. Up close, she looks much younger than Abigail, Jade, and Eleanor. Her wide brown eyes narrow as she purses her lips. "I'm Brea," she says, folding her golden-brown arms across her chest. She looks me up and down as if my jeans and T-shirt are somehow offending her. Like the others, she's dressed in white, but her style is different. It's much more preppy, complete with knee-high socks, tennis shoes, and a headband.

"I'm Cami," says the last one, so quietly that I can barely hear her.

"Speak up, dear," Abigail says, her voice sharp and direct. It reminds me of the way a mother would correct a child.

Cami pinches her shoulders back and clears her throat. "I'm Cami," she repeats, this time meeting my eyes. She wears loose white jeans and a white tank top. Her skin is the lightest of the bunch—so pale that it seems almost as white as her clothes. I'm struck by how young she looks, as though she might not be much older than me, which is ridiculous because how could a teenager live in a house by herself?

"Welcome to the neighborhood," I tell her, because I'm not sure what else to say and it seems polite.

"We won't keep you," Abigail says, gesturing to the street. "I just wanted to make sure that we were acquainted, especially now that the sign is up and everything is official."

"What does it mean?" Mike asks, finally finding his voice.

Abigail blinks at him. "What does *what* mean?"

Mike lowers his Yankees hat, looking even more uncomfortable under her gaze. "What does *Design on Goodie* mean?" He fidgets beside me, something I've never seen him do, not even when talking to the Oldies.

"I own an interior design company," Abigail explains. "The girls and I work together." She smiles at us. "I wouldn't suppose either of you would have any interest in design?

I'm always looking for helpers. You could swing by after school and lend a hand, if you're interested."

"No thanks," I say quickly. "We're both kind of busy with track."

Abigail's eyes seem to darken before she nods. "Of course. But please, spread the word and let us know if you have any friends who'd be interested."

I immediately think of Lex. "Sure," I say.

"In fact, bring them to the party on Sunday," Abigail says, her smile stretching even wider.

"What party?" Mike asks.

Abigail gestures to the sign on her lawn. "We're having an open house to introduce ourselves to the neighborhood and welcome everyone into our home. I hope you both will come. And your parents, of course."

"Will there be food?" Mike asks. I elbow him, but Abigail just laughs.

"Plenty of food. I've already hired the caterer."

"Then we're in," Mike says. I shoot him a look as Abigail claps her hands together.

"Wonderful!"

I start backing away, tugging on Mike's sleeve. "We should really get going. We don't want to be late for school."

"Oh, heck no," Mike says, to my relief, following my lead. "My parents will kill me."

"Nice to meet you," I call over my shoulder.

Abigail arches an eyebrow. "The pleasure was ours."

Mike and I turn on our heels and walk briskly down the street, but I feel eyes on my back until we reach the corner.

Once we're alone, I turn to Mike. "Why in the *world* did you do that?"

"Do what?"

"Tell them we'd go to their stupid party?"

He looks at me. "Parker, she hired a *caterer.*"

"I swear, all you ever think about is your stomach," I mutter. My chest tightens. I don't know why, but going to the party seems like the worst idea in the world.

"What's the big deal?" Mike asks. "It'll be fun."

"How is going to a party with a bunch of adults *fun*?"

He puffs out his chest. "Because you'll be with me."

I laugh, and the tension starts to melt.

"Besides," he continues, adjusting the straps on his backpack, "aren't you curious? Don't you want to see the inside of that house now that Bea's gone?"

He's got me, and he knows it. Grandma Jane always says that curiosity is both a blessing and a curse, and in this case, she may be right.

"Fine," I grunt, kicking a rock across the sidewalk. "I'll go." A cocky smirk spreads across his lips. "Don't look so smug about it."

"I'll pick you up at seven," he says.

"The sign says the party starts at six."

"We can't show up to a party when it starts." With this, he pulls his hat down low over his eyes. "We have to be fashionably late, Parker."

I laugh and swat at the brim of his hat.

"Hey!" he cries, but he's laughing, too, and for a moment I almost forget about our strange encounter with the Ladies in White.

In fact, I don't think about them again until lunch, when I'm surrounded by my girls and reminded of the way Abigail had stared us down on the street after Harvey's.

"What's with you?" Zoe asks, poking me in the nose with her french fry. "Why so moody?"

I swipe at the fry and stuff it in my mouth before Zoe can stop me. She just shrugs and nudges me with her finger. "What's going on, Quinnie?"

"I don't know," I mumble, throwing a look toward Mike at the next table. "I had a weird morning."

"What happened?" Kaylee asks.

"It's nothing, really," I start. "I just met the new neighbors."

Lex gasps. "The one with the incredible dress?"

"What did they do?" Zoe asks.

I squish my sandwich bread between my fingers. "It was kind of . . ." I search for the word. *Strange.*

The girls look at me with widened eyes. "Strange how?"

"Just—I don't know. They were really . . . *polite.*" As soon as I say the word out loud, I realize how stupid it sounds.

"But too polite," I add quickly. "Like they were trying too hard to be nice."

"I don't get it," Zoe says. "Why is that a bad thing?"

"It's not," I admit, shifting in my seat. "Never mind."

Lex leans forward across the table. "But how did they *look*—you know, up close? Did they tell you their names? What else did they say?"

"The one in Bea's house is named Abigail," I answer. "I got the impression that she was the boss. And . . . I don't know. They all looked pretty, I guess."

"What did you talk about?"

"Not much. They just introduced themselves and told us about their open house on Sunday. They asked us to go."

Zoe snorts. "No thanks."

I frown. "Mike already volunteered me."

Zoe waves another fry in my face. "Too. Bad. For. *You*."

"Well, I'm going," Lex says excitedly. "I'm going to have my mom take me. I already picked out my look and everything."

"Why?" Zoe asks. "It sounds like the most boring party in the world."

"It sounds *sophisticated*," Lex says, pushing back her shoulders.

"What else did they say?" Kaylee asks me.

"Yeah, Quinnie. I'm still waiting for the weird part."

"I don't know. Not much. They just told us about the party and then asked if either of us was into interior design or whatever."

Zoe snorts. "They asked *you*? They should see your room."

"My room is nice!" I cry. "Anyway, I told them no. They said they were looking for some kind of after-school help or something, so I just told them Mike and I had track and we couldn't."

Lex grabs my arm. "Are you serious? They're looking for a helper? Like an intern?"

I blink. "I don't think it's anything that serious."

"But they told you they were looking for someone to help out?"

"Yes," I admit, suddenly wishing that I never brought this up. "It's probably really boring, though. Like fluffing their pillows or making sure everything is the perfect shade of white or whatever." I look hard at Lex. "You wouldn't like it."

Lex goes quiet. Even after I try to change the subject, she still looks far away, as if her mind is elsewhere. My stomach tightens as I study her.

Maybe I'm just overreacting, I think. *I should be encouraging her to volunteer with Abigail—it's the kind of thing she'd be great at.*

But I couldn't ignore the feeling that something was wrong about all this.

Either way, I guess Mike agreeing to go to the open house isn't a totally bad thing; maybe it will help me find the answers I'm looking for.

CHAPTER 3

On Sunday night, I can hear the party across the street before it even starts. Billy and I watch the cars line up in a parade of colors, suddenly turning Goodie Lane into the place to be in South Haven. I watch people talk excitedly as they climb Abigail's front steps and ring her doorbell. The outside of the house is lit up from every angle, like a beacon signaling that everyone is welcome.

But something still feels off.

"What do you think, Billy?" I ask, turning my face to his. He licks my nose. "Good assessment," I tell him, before patting him on the head. "Come on. Let's get you a biscuit. I've got to get ready."

"Wear something nice," Mom had told me at dinner. *"Make a good first impression for us Parker women. Especially since I'm working, and Grandma Jane has her dance class with Red."*

I was just planning on wearing a T-shirt and jeans, but it looks as though Mom put an outfit on my bed before she left for the hospital. It's a black sundress with a skater skirt. We'd bought it together during one of our back-to-school shopping trips. When I lift it up, a note falls onto my comforter. The familiar writing reads:

Please don't wear it with your running shoes. And get to bed early. It's a school night. Love you. xoxoxo Mom

Sighing, I hold the dress up in front of the mirror. Well, she said I shouldn't wear my running shoes with it, but she didn't say anything about my Converse.

I get dressed and brush my hair out. For a minute, I actually consider leaving it down before I get annoyed with it in my face and pull it back up into a ponytail. By the time I finish, it's almost seven.

"Bye, Billy," I say, once I'm back downstairs. "I'll be home soon." I purse my lips together and add, "Hopefully . . ."

It's still warm outside, and I feel comfortable enough in my dress and kicks. I stare across the street at Abigail's house. Through the windows, I can see guests filling the space, laughing, having fun. My eyes slide up to the second floor, and something dark takes shape against the glass. A person? A shadow? I squint and step forward, trying to make it out.

"Well, don't we look fancy."

Startled, I spin around, only to find Mike standing behind me, tugging on the bottom of his navy blue button-down. It matches the color of his Yankees hat.

"You dressed up?" I ask.

Mike grins. "For our date."

"You wish it was a date," I say, trying desperately to hide my blush.

He feigns shock, clutching his heart. "But I thought I was your boyfriend? Haven't we been together since last spring?"

"For pre-tend!"

He takes a step closer to me. "Actually, Parker, this is technically our second real date."

I blink. "What are you talking about?"

"The Come as Your Favorite Holiday Dance? You remember?"

Do I remember? How could I forget? I was dressed as a witch to represent Halloween, while Mike was dressed up as some kind of pathetic Christmas tree. We slow-danced, and for a moment we got so close that I thought he might kiss me. But we didn't kiss—not that I wanted him to. Anyway, it doesn't matter. We ended up spending the rest of the dance on opposite sides of the gym.

"That wasn't a date," I mumble, looking away.

Mike steps forward until our sneakers are pointing

toward each other, just an inch or two apart. "You know, we kind of never talked about that night, Parker."

My stomach swirls. "That's because there's nothing to talk about."

"Are you still mad about me leaving you on the dance floor?"

"I'm not mad at anything," I say, my whole body feeling hot under his gaze.

"I only ran away because—"

Suddenly a horn blares behind us, causing us both to jump. The Massiminis, the owners of my favorite pizza place, wave to us from their windows, pulling up in front of Abigail's house. I turn back to Mike standing underneath the streetlight.

"What were you going to say?"

But he's lowered his eyes, as if the horn has woken him up and now he's too embarrassed to say what's on his mind. "Never mind. Let's just go in." With this, he starts off across the street.

My heart sinks a little as I trot to catch up to him. Mr. and Mrs. Massimini have already disappeared into the house. Jazz music spills onto the pavement, along with laughter and loud voices chattering away. After the Oldies, it should come as a relief to see so much life inside this place, but it's unsettling in some way, like dissonant notes in a song.

"Want to peer through the windows first?" Mike jokes. "For old time's sake?"

I nudge him with my elbow, but my eyes automatically scan across the yard. "I wonder what happened to the roses. They're nearly all gone."

"Who cares. They probably died with Bea. Anyway, come on. I smell food." He pulls on my hand, and together we climb the front steps.

The door swings open before Mike can even put his fingers on the handle. Eleanor and Jade smile down on us, standing in the center of a black-and-white-checkered floor. An oversized chandelier hangs above their heads, with ornate gold leaves and branches that twist and turn like vines.

Eleanor and Jade both look beautiful, and for a second, Mike and I are speechless. With their wing-tipped, black eyeliner and glowing cheekbones, they remind me of actresses out of one of Grandma Jane's seventies movies. Both are dressed in white. Once again, Eleanor's in a minidress with billowy sleeves. Jade wears a jumpsuit that scoops at the neck.

"Welcome," they say in unison, their voices rising above the music.

Jade waves her arm toward the adjacent room. "Please make yourselves at home."

"Thanks," Mike manages to say.

Jade and Eleanor turn to greet the next set of guests, their words echoing against the tile: "Welcome."

"This place doesn't look a thing like Bea's," I whisper, my eyes darting around.

Whereas Bea dipped the house in jewel tones and floral prints, Abigail's choices are much more understated and chic. The antique furniture is made of wood that looks expensive. The wallpaper looks textured like the lace on a wedding gown. Fresh flowers are everywhere. I feel like I'm standing in the middle of a magazine.

Except I can't help but notice how cold it is in here. I rub my arms as Mike sniffs the air.

"Food's got to be that way," he says, nodding to a room to the left that is full of people milling around.

"How can you smell anything but flowers?" I ask.

"I have many talents, Parker. Come on."

We pass through an archway and enter a wide-open space that feels like two rooms in one, it's so large. I hadn't thought it was possible to squeeze so many bodies into such a small house, but it seems as if half of South Haven is here.

I spot Brea making her way toward us. She's wearing a white tennis skirt with a sleeveless shirt, and her hair is pulled back into two buns on the top of her head. Mike waves to her, but she doesn't wave back even though she's looking right at him.

I giggle. "Burned!"

"She just didn't see me."

"She definitely saw you."

"No one can ignore this face." He waves bigger, practically stepping in front of Brea. "Hey, remember me? I'm your neighbor, Mike." He flashes a smile that I'm sure he thinks is dazzling.

Her feathered lashes blink slowly. Everything about her expression looks bored and annoyed. She still doesn't bother to answer. I can feel the heat from Mike's embarrassment—I know he's not used to this kind of rejection.

"And I'm Quinn," I add quickly, even though Brea clearly doesn't care.

She looks me up and down just like she did when we met this morning, her sharp eyes taking in my clothes, my hair, my sneakers. I try to stand tall and match her gaze, but before I can get in another word, Jade and Eleanor approach from the side.

The pair look a bit more relaxed away from the door. Their hands are linked together. Eleanor whispers something into Jade's ear that makes Jade burst out laughing.

"Tell Brea," she says, still giggling.

Eleanor slides over to Brea and whispers something to her. Mike and I hang awkwardly on the sidelines, excluded by their inside jokes yet somehow unable to leave the circle. To my surprise, stone-cold Brea bursts out laughing at whatever Eleanor just told her. Her entire face lights up. She looks younger. Happier. Free.

And then Abigail enters the room, bringing a draft with her. Jade and Eleanor stiffen before they scurry back over to their post. The smile disappears from Brea's face as she moves away from us. My eyes shift to Abigail, watching her as she floats from guest to guest, charming everyone with her smile. She's wearing a plain white knee-length dress that somehow doesn't look plain on her, and her blonde hair is down and curled. Her gold necklace catches the light every time she moves.

"This whole party is kind of weird, don't you think?" I whisper to Mike.

"The only thing weird is that my stomach's still empty." His eyes scan the room before landing on an appetizer station in the back. "Yes!" he cries, before making a beeline straight for it.

Grudgingly, I follow him. The food does look good, so I take my own plate, and we both pile them high with fancy-looking tea sandwiches and cubes of cheese. Next, we head down to the drink station, where we fill up crystal glasses with homemade fruit punch.

"I like our new neighbors," Mike says through a mouthful of food.

"Wipe your face," I tell him. "You've got mustard on your chin." I place my drink on the table and hand him a napkin, before stuffing a few extras into the pocket of my dress. I'm picking my drink back up just as Abigail approaches.

"I'm so glad you could make it," she coos, flashing her teeth at Mike and me. She eyes our plates. "And I see you're enjoying the refreshments?"

"So good," Mike mumbles, his mouth still stuffed. I nudge him with my elbow, and he swallows, grinning at Abigail.

"Hi, Cami," I say, noticing her for the first time, hovering behind Abigail.

"Hi," she says, but only after a curt look from Abigail. Like the others, she's dressed all in white, pairing a casual tank top with a short, sequined skirt. She's also wearing a beaded choker with a tiny dragonfly that dangles at her throat. When she catches me looking at it, she scowls in a way that makes the room feel colder. I step closer to Mike, who keeps on eating his food.

"It's a shame your parents couldn't come tonight," Abigail says. "I'd love to meet them. It seems that our schedules never line up."

"Yeah, they're pretty busy," Mike says.

"I was hoping I could have talked to them about the volunteer opportunity," she continues, touching the heart necklace. Up close, I realize that it has a latch—it's a locket! My fingers tingle, itching to know what kind of photograph she keeps hidden inside.

"I thought we were done taking volunteers," Cami says,

causing Abigail to spin her head unnaturally fast. She frowns, and Cami shrinks back immediately.

"Quinn!"

I glance over at the voice to see Lex, weaving through the crowd. She's wearing a plum-colored dress that hits just above the knee, paired with lace-up boots. There's glitter on her lips and in her mussed-up hair. She makes her way over to me, totally unaware of the tension.

Abigail's grimace cracks around the edges to form a smile that she sets on Lex.

"Are you one of Quinn's friends from school?" she asks, extending her hand. "I'm Abigail."

Lex graciously shakes it, grinning from cheek to cheek. "I *know*," she gushes. "I just love your style. This house." She motions around the room. "It's, like, the most stylish thing to happen to South Haven. And your dress—I love it!"

Abigail laughs. "Thank you. You're quite stylish yourself."

Lex blushes at the compliment, and I notice that Abigail is still holding Lex's hand. It feels too personal. I don't like it. Neither does Cami, apparently; when I glance over, she's glaring at Lex.

"Lex, honey, there you are," Mrs. Vega says, approaching. "Oh, hi, Quinn. Hi, Mike. How are you sweeties doing?"

"Hey, Mrs. Vega," we say in unison.

Abigail drops Lex's hand and stiffens. She's still smiling, but the smile looks forced now. "Pleased to meet you," she says.

"You have such a lovely home," Mrs. Vega tells her. "Thank you for inviting us. What a nice way to get all of the neighbors together!"

"Thank you. We want nothing more than to be a part of the community," Abigail says. "I actually was just about to mention a volunteer opportunity to Lex."

"Parker, you've got to try this," Mike says, handing me a sandwich. I push his hand away, focusing on the conversation in front of us.

"You want *me*?" Lex asks, her brows lifting in surprise.

"Well, why not?" Abigail says with a slight laugh. Cami coughs beside her, but Abigail ignores it. "I can already tell that you have a sophisticated eye."

I give Lex the once-over. *Is her style cool? Yes. Very. But sophisticated? I wouldn't go that far. Then again, I don't know any thirteen-year-olds who would* want *to be described that way.*

"And I can see where she gets her style from," Abigail continues, gesturing to Mrs. Vega. "I just adore that dress."

Mrs. Vega runs her fingers over the fabric of her red skirt. Just like Lex, Mrs. Vega loves bright colors. "Oh, I've had this for years," she says, waving her hand.

Lex tugs on her mother's arm. "So can I, Mom?"

"Can you what, honey?"

"Can I volunteer?"

Mrs. Vega presses her painted lips together. "I don't know. I mean, aren't you going to be busy with the school play?"

Abigail's eyes narrow, but her mouth continues to smile—all teeth, like a wolf.

"That's not until the winter, Mom," Lex says. "And I need volunteer hours for my social studies class anyway."

"I don't know," Mrs. Vega says. "I'll have to think about it."

"Please, Mom?"

At this moment, Mrs. Vega's phone chirps from inside her purse. "Oh, it's probably the twins," she says, fumbling around in her bag.

"It's always the twins," Lex mumbles.

"Julian needs me to call him," Mrs. Vega says after reading a text. "Excuse me. I'll be right back." The phone is already to her ear as she walks away. "Julian? Honey, calm down, it's in the dryer. No, not the washer. The *dry-er*."

And just like that, we're left alone with Abigail and Cami. As soon as Mrs. Vega is out of sight, Abigail takes a step closer to Lex, draping an arm around her shoulder. Something about the gesture makes my bones ache.

"Your mother seems awfully busy," Abigail says. "Don't worry. We'll get her to agree. You'll be my volunteer in no time!"

"That would be so amazing," Lex breathes.

"Ugh!" Mike cries, directing our attention toward him. A blob of mustard has fallen onto his shirt. "Parker, can I have one of your napkins?"

I can't help but laugh. "Yeah, sure." But my hands are still full with my plate and drink.

"Parker, hurry, it's staining!"

"Mustard doesn't stain," I tell him.

"Tell that to my shirt."

I turn to Cami. "Can you hold my glass?" Before waiting for an answer, I hand it to her, noticing a second too late that she's not looking at me; her eyes are still burning toward Lex. She turns to me and reaches out her hand just in the nick of time, but the glass goes straight through her palm, crashing onto the ground. The crystal shatters into a million different directions, causing a couple of jumps and screams from the other guests. For a long moment, everything feels frozen, like time itself has stopped.

Then Mr. Camarro, the hardware store owner, yells out, "Party foul!" and a chorus of laughs follow.

The chatter picks back up as guests step around the glass, as if everything is normal. But everything is so not normal. Cami's hand was translucent! She didn't miss the glass—it fell *through* her hand. Through skin and bone and tissue.

I stare at her with my jaw hanging open. But now she's looking at Abigail, who's gazing back with tight lips, her face inexplicably covered in shadow despite the blinding lights in the room.

"Clean it up, Camille," she hisses, barely moving her mouth.

For the first time all evening, Cami looks afraid. "Right away," she says, scurrying out of the room.

It takes Abigail a beat to compose herself, but then the shadows seem to melt, and she steers Lex away to a different corner of the room. Cami returns with a dustpan and a broom. She glares at me as I sheepishly hand Mike a pile of napkins.

"Man, it's ruined," he mumbles, pouting at his shirt.

"I think it's time to leave," I tell him.

With this, I set my plate down on the closest table, and we head back to the front door.

Jade and Eleanor are still there, standing so close that their shoulders touch. "See you soon," they say as one in this sing-song voice that sends chills up my spine.

I just nod and push Mike through the door and down the steps, until we're finally alone on the dark street.

"Parker, what's with you?" he asks, once we're in my driveway. "Are you *that* worried about my shirt?" He grins. "I look good in this shirt, don't I?"

"Yes—no. Ugh, Mike, just listen!" I realize that I'm breathing heavily. "Something happened back there."

He smirks. "Yeah. You broke a glass. A pretty expensive-looking one, too. Way to impress our new neighbors, Parker."

"It went straight through her hand!"

"Because you have bad aim."

"No, I mean it went *through* her hand. Not in between her fingers. Her palm went totally clear."

He raises an eyebrow, "Are you feeling OK? I know it was hectic in there, but I don't think—"

"I know what I saw, Mike!"

"You know what you *think* you saw."

Before I can answer, a cold wind rushes around us, flipping my ponytail up over my head. A shadow hovers behind Mike for a moment. But when I blink, it's gone.

"Did you see that?" I ask, spinning around.

Mike's no longer smirking. Instead, his lips tighten with concern. "I think we should call it a night, Parker. You seem kind of tired."

I start to protest, but then I force a shrug. "Maybe you're right."

He narrows his eyes. "You sure you're OK?"

"Fine," I lie, still feeling the wind in my hair.

"OK," he says. "I'll see you in the morning. Nice and early!"

"Night, Mike."

"Goodnight, Parker."

We both make our way over to our respective houses. I hover on the top step for a moment, squinting at Abigail's house across the street, its windows still lit up like a jack-o'-lantern. My eyes scan up to the top floor, where I remember seeing the dark shape from earlier, but all seems quiet now. Sighing, I head inside.

Billy greets me at the door. "Hey, boy," I tell him, patting his head. "Come on. We've got work to do." Then I bribe him with a biscuit to follow me upstairs.

Once in my bedroom, I change into my pajamas and open my laptop. I don't know what to type into the search bar, so I just enter the question that's on my mind: **objects going through people?** To my surprise, a bunch of hits populate the screen. Most of them are physics articles. *Mike would love this*, I think. I start clicking around and skimming the pages. They're hard to understand—something about quantum tunneling that's *way* beyond my middle school science expertise—but I'm able to get the gist of one.

Can Humans Walk through Walls? the headline reads. My eyes hover over one line in particular: In theory, if our molecules perfectly align with a wall's molecules, we should be able to walk through walls. However, due to our size, this makes it statistically impossible.

I frown. Impossible? But I just saw it happen! Well, sort of . . . Maybe I need a different search.

"What should I try next, Billy?" He flops down onto a corner of the area rug, closing his eyes on impact. "Well, you're no help," I mumble.

I think for a minute, chewing on my bottom lip. Maybe I need something more specific? Shrugging, I type in a statement: **hands becoming see-through**. This time, I get a bunch of medical articles about a rare skin condition.

"That wasn't it," I tell the screen. "Cami doesn't have a skin condition . . ."

I keep scrolling, losing interest as nothing relevant pops up. But just when I'm ready to throw in the towel, one word catches my eye at the bottom of the screen: *GHOST*. I click on it, sucking in my breath as I read the headline: **The Science on Ghosts.** I start reading:

Ghosts are disembodied souls that the living can see, feel, or hear. Oftentimes, the apparitions linger when they have unfinished business, something that's still tying them to the world of the living. Sometimes a sudden death holds them; sometimes they just want to let their loved ones know that they're OK.

I stiffen in my seat, my eyes flickering over to Dad's photo on my dresser. I keep reading.

Evidence has proven that ghosts take on many different forms.

Really? I hadn't known there were different kinds of ghosts. I grab a notebook and a pen out of my desk drawer and begin to make a list, copying the information from off the screen.

Funnel ghosts are the most common type. The living

often describe an encounter with a funnel ghost as a sudden cold spot in a room.

Orbs are the second most common, most often seen in photographs. Orbs look like spots of floating light. They're usually circular, but sometimes they take the shape of a person. Nonbelievers will always try and claim that the orbs are just a camera trick, or something wrong with the flash, but they have a harder time explaining orbs that don't appear in photographs, when one is following them in a graveyard.

I shiver as I write, my handwriting looking scrawled and messy.

Ectoplasm is when the ghost takes a more physical form, like a liquid substance, mist, fog, or shadows.

I gulp as I reread the last word, remembering the shadows in Abigail's window.

And finally, we have poltergeists. Despite what the movies want us to believe, poltergeists are the rarest form of ghosts. They are otherwise known as the "noisy" ghost. As the haunting intensifies, they can manipulate and move objects, even throw heavy furniture across a room. Poltergeists are the only truly dangerous form of ghosts.

Suddenly, my laptop screen starts to blink. "What the . . ."

A shadow stretches up the wall in front of me, causing a chill to seep into my skin. I stare up at it, totally frozen. But then, just like that, the shadow disappears. The computer screen hums and then returns to normal.

Billy jolts up and barks, running to my window. His nose points toward it, as if sensing something outside.

"What's up, bud?"

I rub away the goosebumps on my arms as I walk over to him. I squint across the street. Cars are still parked outside Abigail's. Guests are starting to trickle out, though, and as the front door opens, I catch a glimpse of the Ladies in White inside the foyer, their feet planted on the checkered floor. Cami's eyes meet mine for a split second, only hers look hollow and black, like two tunnels drilled into her skull. I gasp and step back, nearly tripping over Billy.

"Sorry, boy."

I force myself to take a slow, deliberate breath before peering back through the glass. Only now, the door across the street is closed.

CHAPTER 4

I dream about ghosts all night. Crystal orbs floating around, morphing into faces with dark eyes like Cami's. Then the orbs stretch out and grow, sliding up my walls like liquid, until the curved edges sharpen into knives.

When I wake up, I'm covered in sweat, and Billy is nudging me with his wet nose, his fluffy tail wagging behind him. My alarm clock is going off. I hadn't even heard it, I was in such a deep, awful sleep. I swipe it off and start changing quickly for my run.

Downstairs, I grab the leash, holding it out to Billy. "Want to come with us?"

He answers with an excited little bark. I hook his collar before opening the front door.

For the second school day in a row, Mike is outside before me. My legs want to launch toward him so that I can spill about my dream, the shadows, and the ghost research from last night.

"Hey," I call, guiding Billy over to the driveway. "You're early again."

Billy wags his tail as Mike stoops down to greet him. "Hey, buddy," he says, addressing my dog before looking at me. "Sup, Parker." That's it. No flip of my ponytail, no pat on the back, no cocky smile. Just: *Sup, Parker.*

"You OK?" I ask, stepping back to look at him.

He shrugs and scratches the back of his neck. His hat is so low that I can't see his eyes or read his expression, but he has dark circles under his lids, as if he didn't sleep well last night.

"I'm fine," he mutters. "Just kind of tired."

"Yeah. Me too." I want to keep going, to tell him everything on my mind, but something in his face stops me. After all, we're both tired. Maybe this isn't the right moment for ghost talk.

Billy starts whimpering at my side and tugging at his leash. Mike looks at him. "Is he actually going to run?" he asks. "I thought your mom said he's too old."

I bite my lip. "Yeah, I know. He just looked kind of lonely, so I thought I'd let him come. I can bring him back inside, though."

"No, don't," Mike says, taking the leash from me. "It's cool. We can just walk him."

"You sure?"

"Yeah, we can't tease him like that." Billy flashes Mike a look of love so genuine, I can't help but smile.

"All right. Let's go."

We lap the entire neighborhood twice without the usual banter or competition. When we finally make our way home, Mike and I disappear into our own houses without a word spoken between us.

Mike still looks grumpy when we meet up an hour later to walk to school.

"Hey," he mumbles as he trots down the porch steps, slinging his backpack over his shoulders.

"Hey." I offer him a small smile that he doesn't return, and I can't help but to take it personally. "You sure you're OK?"

"I'm fine."

We start walking toward the sidewalk just as Abigail's front door swings open. She steps outside, looking as beautiful as ever. She waves to us.

"Good morning, kids!"

Mike waves back as I stand frozen in place. "Hi," he says. I can't help but notice that he offers *her* a smile.

She cuts across her lawn until she reaches the **DESIGN ON GOODIE** sign. "Don't need this anymore," she says, pulling the **OPEN HOUSE** piece off its hook. "Hope you both had fun last night."

"I'm sorry I broke your glass," I tell her, feeling my cheeks redden with the words.

She tilts her head to one side and smiles. "Don't even worry about it. I'm just glad I got to meet your friend."

"You mean Lex?"

She nods. "She's going to make such a wonderful addition to the design team."

My lungs suddenly feel too full to respond.

But Abigail just smiles at us. "Well, I'll let you both get on to school. Bye, now." She turns on her flats and makes her way back into the house, closing the door behind her.

"Nice apology," Mike says.

"Shut up," I mumble.

We begin to follow the winding sidewalk along an otherwise empty Goodie Lane.

I can't hold it in any longer. "I don't like her," I blurt out once we turn onto Main Street.

Mike blinks. "Who?"

"Abigail."

"What? Why? She's nice."

"She's fake."

"Come on, Parker. Give her a chance."

"I'm telling you, Mike, something's off about these women, I can feel it."

At this, Mike snorts. "I'm telling *you*, Parker—it's probably just hypervigilance. It happens to some people after they experience trauma. Their body goes on high alert, even if there's no real danger."

"I haven't been through any trauma."

"The Oldies?"

I sigh. "So, you think I'm overreacting?"

"Yes." He nods his head. "Most definitely."

I grip the straps of my backpack so hard that my knuckles turn white. "Forget it." I pick up my pace, jetting ahead of him.

"Parker, wait," he calls, jogging to catch up. "Come on, don't be like that." He tugs on the back of my bag, causing me to slow down.

We fall into place with each other, our shadows stretching out in front of us like giants. I think about last night and the way the glass slipped through Cami's skin as if she were made of air. I think about her empty eyes and the way that she glared so hard at Lex. I think of the shadows that followed me home, dancing on the wall.

Are there really such things as ghosts?

But what if Mike's right? What if I am being paranoid, or hyper-whatever-he-said? What if I'm overreacting, and making something out of nothing? What if our new neighbors are actually totally normal?

My head begins to ache as we continue to walk. The only sound between us is our sneakers snapping against the sidewalk. Neither of us speaks until we come face-to-face with the front of our school. I stop short just before we reach the door and look at Mike.

"Do you believe in ghosts?" I ask, my voice low and hesitant.

It takes Mike a long time to answer, so long that I don't think he ever will. "No," he finally says, drawing out the single syllable so that it sounds like three. *No-o-o.* He turns to me. "You're not having another one of your supernatural theories, are you, Parker?"

I shrug. "Why not? The last one turned out to be right."

He shakes his head. "Still can't believe I let you win that bet."

"*Let* me win? Oh please!"

"I mean, I miss investigating with you and everything. But you know there's no such thing as ghosts, right?"

I inhale sharply. *With me. He misses investigating* with me.

"Well, I want to find out for sure," I tell him. "So, are you in?"

Mike looks me dead in the eyes. "In on a ghost hunt? Nope. No, I'm not."

I wait a full beat before making a face. "Thanks for nothing, Robin," I mutter.

Mike shoves open the double doors of the school. "Still not Robin."

I shrug. "Once a Robin, always a Robin."

"Whatever, Parker. Later." He flashes one last smirk before stepping into the crowd. I watch him until his Yankees hat disappears from sight, then I make my way to my own locker.

I just begin to spin the combination when Lex appears at my side. "You scared me!" I gasp, placing a hand over my heart.

Lex laughs and falls against the locker next to mine. Something looks different about her: at first, I can't figure out what, but then I notice the color—or rather, the *lack* of color.

"What's with all the white?" I ask, the hair on my arms rising with the question.

Lex fans out the bottom of her shirt. "You like?"

"Not sure."

At this, Lex raises her eyebrows. "I thought I'd try something new," she explains. "I'm always wearing bright colors. I thought it was time for a more mature look."

I blink. "It's *different . . .*"

Lex's normal style usually consists of adding every shade of the rainbow to every outfit, and just last week she was begging her mom to let her dye her hair lavender. *Bold*: that's the first word that would come to mind when standing face-to-face with Lex. She's taller and curvier than most of the other eighth graders. Blending in has never been part of her DNA, and the Lex I know has grown up embracing all of the things that make her unique. She's confident, *fearless*.

Today, though, I'm struggling to find even one word to pin-point how it feels to see Lex dressed up like my neighbors.

"Nice," I force myself to add. "You look nice."

Lex glows with the compliment. "You think I look Goodie good?"

I raise my eyebrows. "What's *Goodie good*?" And then I freeze as the realization slowly washes over me.

"You know—Design on Goodie." Lex runs a hand through her short hair, mussing it up so that it somehow looks even more fashionable. "I'm starting my internship today. Mom agreed."

I slam my locker shut a little bit harder than I mean to. "It's not an internship."

"OK, well, I'm starting my *volunteer* hours today."

"Cool," I mutter, before starting off for homeroom.

Lex trots to catch up to me. "Hey, slow down!" she cries, tugging me by the arm and stopping me before we get to Mr. Feagin's door. "What's your problem?"

I feel a heaviness press against me. I don't know what to do; should I tell her my suspicions? Or is this just me being paranoid, like Mike said?

"I don't have a problem," I lie, but my voice sounds unconvincing even to myself. "It's just . . ." I think for a moment. "Is your mom really fine with you spending your afternoons with some random person you just met?"

"She wouldn't even notice. Theater boot camp has

officially begun." She rolls her eyes, and slumps down into her seat. "Winter play, remember?"

I fall into the chair beside her. "It's still kind of weird," I say.

Lex looks at me. "Do *you* want to be their volunteer?"

I almost laugh out loud at the idea of it. "No, I can't think of anything *less* I'd want to do."

"Then what's the problem, Quinn?"

She leans in closer to me; I can smell her melon-scented lotion, and the fancy conditioner that she uses in her hair. She smells familiar, and safe—just like the girl I grew up with. Except this version of my friend looks defeated.

"It's fine," she says with a half-hearted shrug when I don't respond. "I just won't do it then."

The sparkle seems to fade from her eyes, and I feel my guard softening. "No, I'm sorry. You should do it." I swallow and add, "Abigail's lucky to have you."

At this, Lex squeals. "You think so?"

I nod as she continues to ramble away, chasing her own words like butterflies.

It probably is a great opportunity, I tell myself. *A chance to learn about a job that she's been fascinated by since she was a little girl. Lex will be perfect for the role, and what's more, she's going to love it.*

Then why can't I seem to untie the knot that is slowly forming in my stomach?

To my relief, the bell rings, and I dart away from Lex as soon as we dip back into the congested hallway.

"Keep it moving, people," the teachers advise, motioning to us with their hands. "Keep walking. Don't stop."

"Yeah, Quinnie, *keep it moving*," Zoe teases, appearing at my side. Together, we push through the crowd on our way to Spanish class.

Señora Tombline welcomes us with a chipper *Hola* as we take our seats. Jess, my track co-captain, rushes up to me as soon as she arrives.

"Coach wants us to start leading the drills during warm-ups," she says, barking the statement without so much as a *hello* or a *what's up?*

"Good morning to you, too," Zoe mutters, causing me to nudge her beneath the desk.

Jess doesn't even register the sarcasm. She tucks herself into the desk beside me, her eyes narrowed as she leans in close. "I was thinking that we can alternate days. Like you lead one day, I lead the next. Cool?"

I shrug. "Cool."

Jess's face relaxes as she settles back into her chair. "OK, good. I'll tell Coach that I'll start today." She drops her gaze onto her notebook as she begins to doodle little lines and squares.

"OK clase, siéntate," Señora Tombline begins. "Abre tus Chromebooks en tus páginas de Quizlet . . ."

We all take out our computers and pull up the online flash-card-making site. Señora Tombline instructs us to use the period to create flash cards to help us study for our quiz tomorrow so that Señora can see what we remember from last year. I sigh and follow directions, dropping vocabulary words into the appropriate boxes one by one, my eyes feeling heavy in the process, until the sentences become one big blur and lose their meaning.

See, Mike? I can't help but think. *I'm* not *hypervigilant. If I was, I would be way more focused.*

I open a new tab and type the word *hypervigilant* into the keyboard, hitting each key so hard that Zoe leans over and whispers for me to ease up. A slew of links trickle down the screen. I click on the first one and start skimming the page: Hypervigilance is a state of increased alertness . . . always on the lookout for danger . . . symptoms include anxiety . . . I sit back in my seat, realizing that hypervigilance has nothing to do with focus, and everything to do with fear. In fact, the articles suggest that someone who's hypervigilant becomes so focused on finding danger that they distract themselves from real life. *That's not me,* I think, but even still, I close the tab quickly, my hands still hovering over the keys.

Suddenly my fingertips begin typing again; it's like they have a mind of their own, and I barely have time to realize what's happening until my screen reads: DESIGN ON

GOODIE. The home page consists of a simple black-and-white color scheme, with a quote written below the header: *Forever—is composed of nows.*

"What?" I mutter out loud before I can bite my tongue. Zoe turns to me. I immediately try to hide my screen, but it's too late.

"Cool! Is that your neighbors' site? Let me see." She tugs my laptop toward her.

"No, wait—"

"Check it out. They seem legit." Zoe nods to the bio page, wallpapered with tasteful pictures of the Ladies in White. "It says they moved from California to Massachusetts, to New Mexico, to here." She looks at me. "I wonder why they've moved so much. Do you think all five of them move together, or just Abigail?"

I shrug. "I have no idea." *But I'm going to find out.*

Zoe's question follows me all the way to track practice and all the way through Jess's warm-up, until Coach lines us up for sprints.

"Remember, this isn't a race," he tells us, pairing Jess and me together. "This is just to get some times on the books."

Jess and I both nod, and off we all go on Coach's whistle. Just as I start to feel the rhythm of the motions, a shadow overtakes mine on the track, as Jess tears ahead.

"We're not racing," I call to her.

"We're always racing," she answers back, propelling her legs forward.

I feel my heart pounding as I try and catch up.

"Hey, Parker! Wait!" Mike calls after practice, trotting to catch up to me on the hill. "Why are you in such a hurry?"

"I don't know," I mutter. "Jess was annoying."

"Whatever. It's just practice. You can beat her in a race, no contest."

I sigh. "I thought we were cool at the end of last season. But now she's, like, more competitive than ever."

He pats my shoulder condescendingly. "Don't worry, Parker, it happens to the best of us. I know it's hard to believe, but even *I'm* wrong sometimes."

At this, I laugh. "Yeah, and last time it cost you thirty milkshakes." I smile, remembering our bet about the Oldies, and how I ordered the most luxurious, expensive milkshakes after Mike lost, forcing him to grumble and pay for every single one.

We turn onto our street, and just as the row of white homes come into view, I have an idea.

"Want to put your money where your mouth is again?"

Mike looks at me. "You mean another bet?"

I nod.

"But what do we have to bet on?"

"Our new neighbors."

"Care to be more specific?" Then he shakes his head. "Never mind. Don't say it—"

"*Ghosts.*"

Mike laughs. "You make it too easy, Parker. No—I can't let you do that to yourself. Abigail literally touched my shoulder."

"So?"

"*So*, I don't believe in ghosts, but even if I did, I'm pretty sure they can't touch people."

"Poltergeists can," I insist.

He shakes his head. "Parker, come on."

"What? If you don't believe me, why not just take the bet? Scared you'll owe me another month's worth of milkshakes, Robin?"

"Never."

"So, are you in, or are you out?"

Mike's eyes twinkle in the sun. "Oh, I'm *all* in. Just name your terms."

"How about we mix it up a little this time," I suggest. "Like, instead of buying each other milkshakes, we up the stakes?"

Mike thinks for a moment before a smile creeps across his lips. "OK, I got it. The winner gets to pick a costume for the loser to wear."

I make a face. "To do *what* in?"

"Run. During a *track* meet."

My jaw drops. "Are you kidding? Coach will kill us!"

"What are you so worried about?" he teases. "You just said a minute ago that you're never going to lose."

"I'm not."

"So, do you accept the bet?"

I scowl at him but stick out my hand. "You're on." I shake his sweaty fingers and feel a little buzz of electricity. Quickly, I drop his hand and look away before he can see me blush.

"Hey," Mike says, looking past me, toward our street. "What's *she* doing here?"

I follow his gaze and gasp as my eyes settle on Lex, stepping over the curb of the cul-de-sac, having just come from the direction of the pond. Her entire body seems to glow.

"She's volunteering for Abigail. Don't you remember last night?" I wave my arms in the air. "Lex! Hey, over here!"

But she just keeps walking, as though she doesn't hear me. Her steps are light and airy, and she practically floats across the street to Abigail's house.

"Lex?"

She still doesn't answer me. I hold my breath as I watch her knock on the door, only to be greeted a moment later by Abigail, who smiles graciously before inviting Lex into her home.

"Lex!" I call one last time, but my friend disappears inside. Abigail looks at me and offers a wink before closing the door behind her.

I hear Mike expel a deep breath beside me. I turn to him.

"I sure hope you can run in a tutu," I say.

CHAPTER 5

The next morning, I'm up way before my alarm goes off.

"What's with you, Early Bird?" Mom asks, surprising me in the kitchen. She's wearing her scrubs and nursing a cup of coffee. I spot a tired-looking Billy resting at her feet.

"Couldn't sleep. So I thought I'd just get ready for my run a little early." I slide into the seat beside her. "Why are you up?"

"Shift starts in an hour," she says. "Do you want breakfast?"

I shake my head. "I'll eat after my run."

Mom nudges me with her elbow. "Are you meeting Michael out there? Is that why you have such a cute running outfit on?"

"What cute running outfit?" I cry. "Oh, you mean because I match for once?" I feel my cheeks burn as I look down at the seafoam-green and gray tank top and shorts, tracing my fingers over the stretchy cotton fabric.

Mom shrugs. "It's just nice to see the two of you still spending so much time together. That's all."

"It's not like this is a new thing," I argue. "We've been running together since June."

Mom sips her coffee. "It's just nice."

Before I can answer, the lights flicker on and off, on and off, humming softly above our heads.

"It did it yesterday, too," Mom says, shaking her head. "Not sure what's wrong."

"Maybe we need to change the bulbs?"

"I just did last night."

Weird. Both of us continue to stare up at the fixture, daring the lights to dim again. When they don't, Mom shrugs. "Maybe it's a faulty wire or something. I'll look at it over the weekend." She turns back to her coffee.

A shadow flickers behind her bent head, stretching its wings out as if to embrace her. My chest tightens as I remember my ghost research and the "unfinished business" that the article mentioned. Sometimes they want their loved ones to know they're OK . . .

"You heading out?" Mom asks, startling me back into the moment.

I nod and move toward the door, grabbing the dog leash from off the hook. "Yeah. Come on, Billy."

Billy raises his head once to give me an *I don't think so* look, before dropping his sleepy face back onto the hardwood floor.

Mom reaches over and pats his head. "I think that's a 'no' from Billy."

I glance back to Billy one more time. "Come on, boy. Walk? Walk?"

This time Billy closes his eyes.

"He's old, honey," Mom says. "Let him rest."

"Maybe next time, bud," I tell Billy. His peaceful snore follows me out the door.

As soon as I step out onto the street, I gasp. "You're early again?" I cry, jumping at the sight of Mike hovering on my driveway. "How is this possible?"

"I wonder that all the time," Mike answers. He gestures to himself. "I mean, how is this much perfection possible in one person?" He flashes his signature cocky smile, but the sparkle is gone from his eyes—eyes that are once again lined with deep, dark circles that I can see despite his hat being so low.

"Are you sure you're OK?" I ask.

"Never better," he says, beginning to stretch out his quads. "Why do you ask me that every day?"

"Because you look like death," I reply, meaning it as a joke.

Mike frowns. "Well, you're not so hot yourself," he snaps.

I shrink back at his words. After a moment, I silently begin stretching beside him, wishing I was able to hide behind my ponytail. I feel him come over to me, but I still don't look up.

"Hey, I'm sorry—I . . ." He trails off and sighs. "I'm just tired. I haven't been sleeping that great. I've been having these . . ." He stops again, as if summoning up the courage to say the last word. "Nightmares."

At this, I look up. "Nightmares?"

Mike nods.

"About what?" I ask, when he doesn't elaborate.

He shifts in his sneakers, tugging on the rim of his hat with shaky hands. "I don't really want to talk about it."

"Are they about the Oldies?"

He gives a stiff nod, not looking at me. I think about our former neighbors, about the horrific way that they burned right there in front of us, not far from where we're standing now. The scene is impossible to forget, and I don't blame Mike one bit for dreaming about it.

"When did they start?" I ask him gently.

"A couple of days ago." He then puffs out his chest and shakes his arms out. "Look, Parker, I really don't want to talk about it. Can we just run?"

"Sure." I quickly glance over at Abigail's quiet house across the street before jetting after Mike, who, to my surprise, takes off toward the pond.

"You sure you want to go this way?" I ask, pulling up to his side.

Mike's face is determined. "Nothing to be scared of. The Oldies are dead, remember?"

I nod and follow him through the trees until we break out to the clearing. The pond is nestled within an old stone wall covered in moss, surrounded by thin, aging trees that rise up with their claw-like branches reaching for the sun. I've always found this place to be creepy—even before the Oldies, even before I saw the witch's face watching me from below the surface, and the orange glow tempting me under. Maybe it's because the water is so thick and still; it's hard to tell what's lurking beneath. Or maybe it's because the air always feels a little cooler here, like the wind is whispering a warning on the back of your neck.

I shiver and run faster.

Mike and I extend our run a little longer than usual. I guess we both need the distraction. By the time I make it back home, Mom has already left for her shift at the hospital. I kick off my sneakers and leave them by the stairs, before jogging up to my room. I barely have enough time to shower and get dressed before the alarm on my phone buzzes, demanding that I get out the door.

I look for my running shoes where I left them at the foot of the stairs, only they're not there. I search the kitchen and the living room: nothing! *Where are they?* Just as I start to feel the frustration in my muscles, I hear Billy's collar jingle as he stretches out on his bed. My shoes are right beside him, in the same spot where Dad used to keep his own sneakers. I approach them cautiously, as if they've somehow come alive and walked themselves over here.

"Billy, did you?" But I don't finish my sentence. *That's ridiculous. Billy hasn't moved. I was upstairs. Mom isn't home. That leaves only one explanation . . .*

"Hey, Parker, come on!" Mike suddenly calls from the other side of the door.

I hop on one foot at a time while I lace up my shoes, before saying goodbye to Billy and joining Mike outside.

The walk to school is quiet as Mike conserves what's left of his energy, and I get lost in my own thoughts. *What's really going on here? What's up with the shadows, the lights, my sneakers? Does it all connect to the Ladies in White? And if it does, how? Why?*

I keep an eye on their houses as we lumber down Goodie Lane. Unlike the Oldies, who were always outside by the crack of dawn, the Ladies in White are nowhere to be seen this morning. I can't decide whether this is normal or strange, but regardless, there was definitely something unsettling about the wink Abigail gave me yesterday when Lex entered her house. *Lex.* I bite my lip as Mike and I walk, picturing my friend in her pale ensemble, practically skipping into the house of a stranger. *What was she thinking?*

My spirits lift a little as we turn onto Main Street. Mike kicks a rock toward me, and we pass it back and forth the entire way to Rocky Hill.

"Oh shoot, we're late!" Mike says, glancing at his phone.

The two of us run inside the building, barreling down the nearly empty hallway just as the homeroom bell rings.

"See you, Parker," he cries, ducking into his room.

"Bye!"

Mr. Feagin raises his eyebrows as I slide into my seat. "You just made it," he says, turning back to his computer.

"Hey, Quinn," Lex says, patting the seat beside her. I can't help but notice that she's looking even more put together than usual in white skinny jeans and a white linen T-shirt. The combination somehow makes her look older yet younger at the same time, like she's trying too hard to dress like a grown-up. What's more, her skin seems to be glowing, her eyes large and bright as though she just had the most wonderful sleep.

"Morning!" she chirps, offering a wide smile. "Got you this." She pushes an iced tea toward me; it's from our favorite coffee shop.

"Wow, thanks," I say gratefully, lifting the drink off the desk. "What's this for?"

Lex holds her own iced coffee out for us to clink our plastic cups. "Just a thank-you. You know, for hooking me up with Abigail."

I almost spit out my tea. "I didn't do anything. That was all you."

"Is it weird that I'm still nervous? I mean, Abigail is cool and everything, but I don't know if the others like me. Especially Cami."

Just thinking about those glaring eyes makes me straighten in my seat. But before I can answer, Lex shakes her head.

"No—forget it. I'm just being paranoid. They were all nice yesterday. I'm going to be fine."

"Definitely," I tell her, even though it feels like she's trying to convince herself of this more than me.

Luckily, the bell rings, and I don't have to say much more as we separate for our first-period classes. I don't see her again until lunch, and we spend the entire time consoling Zoe about her bad grade on her art project, so I don't get the chance to ask Lex my questions about Cami. I don't see her again for the rest of the day.

By the time practice rolls around, my shoulders feel tight with worry. I remember the angry way that Cami stared at Lex during the open house, right before the glass broke. If

Cami *is* a ghost, then, according to my research, she must be a poltergeist—the kind that can touch and move objects. The kind that may also be dangerous.

"Let's go, girls, huddle up!" Jess cries, blowing a whistle that I didn't realize she had. It looks a lot like the one hanging around Coach's neck, and I catch him nodding to her approvingly. "Let's start with windmills, come on!" She starts swinging her arms around in circles, and I watch in shock as my teammates follow her.

I jog over to her. "I thought it was my day to lead," I whisper.

She doesn't even look at me. "Was it?"

"Yeah, you led the warm-ups yesterday."

She juts her chin out. "Didn't think you were up to it. You weren't on the field." She blows her whistle again. "High knees!"

Before I can answer, Coach claps his hands. "Parker! Get moving. Just because you're a captain doesn't mean you get to skimp out of the work."

I feel my cheeks redden before I fall into line, attacking each drill with everything I've got. As if practice couldn't be going any worse, Coach pairs me off against Jess for sprints.

"Parker! Pace yourself!" Coach barks. "This is just a drill."

This so not a drill, I think, glaring at Jess as I sprint even faster.

Mike is waiting for me by the fence at the end of practice. I must look like a total wreck as I practically crawl toward him, my ponytail half-out, my body drenched with sweat. I'm so hot that my skin burns.

Mike blinks. "What happened to you?"

"Jess took over."

"Parker, you can't let her walk all over you. You have to take charge—show her who is boss." He makes a face. "Well, co-boss."

"I tried . . ." I trail off, remembering the way Jess steam-rolled me in front of the team, blowing her stupid whistle, trying to copy Coach. I look down at my sneakers. "Maybe I'm not cut out for captain."

Mike thrusts a water bottle toward me. "Here."

"What's this for?"

"You're dehydrated. I mean, you must be, because what you just said is ridiculous."

"I'm not ridiculous," I grumble, but I take the water and chug. I feel the cool liquid flowing through my entire body, waking up my limbs. I won't admit it to Mike, but I do feel kind of better. "Thanks," I tell him, handing him back his bottle. "I don't get it," I continue. "I don't remember her being like this last season."

Mike tucks his bottle back into his bag and slows down

his pace so that we fall into step with each other. "That's because you were a little distracted last season." He shrugs. "Don't worry. It'll get easier. You just have to be persistent. Jess will cave—I've seen her do it."

"Really?"

"Yup. We were lab partners in sixth-grade science. Didn't you know that?"

"How would I know that?"

He waves a hand. "Doesn't matter. Point is, she tried to take over every single experiment, until one day I just didn't give her the chance, and I took the lead. That's the only lab we got an A on. The next day, she begged Mr. McCabe to switch partners."

"Wow," I breathe. "She really does hate to lose."

Mike shrugs. "She's not all bad. I mean, she's not, like, Oldies evil or anything." He winks at me as we turn onto Goodie Lane.

Together, we glide past the first three houses, Abigail's, Eleanor and Jade's, then Brea's, before skidding to a stop in front of the fourth house, the one owned by Cami. We watch as Cami storms out of her home, slamming the door behind her.

"Wow," Mike says, following my gaze. "She does *not* look happy."

"Definitely not," I agree.

We watch as she cuts across her lawn toward Abigail's house. Abigail suddenly appears at her front door, her arm linked with Lex's. My whole body stiffens as I strain my ears to hear their chatter, which falls between their high-pitched laughs. Abigail notices Cami and hands her what looks like a purse, before moving right past her toward the car in the driveway. Lex takes the front seat, sitting right next to Abigail. Cami hovers in the grass clutching Abigail's purse, staring hard at Lex through the window. Abigail then beeps the horn, signaling for Cami to get in. With this, Cami slides into the backseat, and the three of them take off down the street. Lex notices me and waves before they disappear.

"That was . . ." Mike starts, his words trailing off.

"Strange?" I ask, eyeing him. "Admit it. Something's up."

Mike turns and moseys toward his house. "You keep telling yourself that, Parker."

"Pretty soon you're going to lose another bet, Michael Warren!" I call after him.

I can hear his exaggerated laughter even after he goes inside.

CHAPTER 6

Cami's eyes haunt me for the rest of the evening, all the way through to the next morning as I dress for my run. It's almost as though Cami had wanted Lex to disappear yesterday. I flip through the notebook on my desk and reread the entry about poltergeists: **Poltergeists are the only truly dangerous form of ghosts.**

Could my new neighbor be a threat to one of my best friends? I need to find out for sure. And I need to get Mike on board to investigate.

I shoot a quick glance at the time and then sigh. I can't let Mike beat me outside again. I gather my hair into a ponytail and check my backpack for my house key. Mom's already at the hospital, so I need to zip it in the pocket of my running shorts. But I can't find it—it's not in my back-pack, or my coat, or yesterday's jeans, or in the kitchen, or anywhere. I wonder if I dropped it on the track or somewhere at school.

Billy senses my stress and nuzzles his sweet face against my leg. I stoop down to pet him, and when I stand back up, I see it: my key! Sitting on my dresser right beside my favorite framed photograph of Dad. I shake my head, picking it up. *But I looked here already*, I think. Dad's picture smiles back at me, and for a second, I swear I see him wink through the glass. I gasp and drop the key onto the carpet. Billy lets out a low growl. I shush him and pick up the picture, squinting at it, turning it over in my hands. Nothing seems to be out of the ordinary—just a regular old picture in a regular old frame. My fingers tremble as I place the picture back down and pick up my key. Suddenly the room feels cold, as if I'd left the window open all night during a rainstorm. I do a double check, but the glass is pulled tightly closed. My eyes flicker to my notebook: **Funnel ghosts are often described as a cold spot in a room** . . .

I think I need to get out of here.

"Come on, boy," I say to Billy, trying to keep my voice even. "Let's get you a biscuit." I look over my shoulder one last time just to be sure that everything's as it should be. Then together we bound down the stairs.

As promised, I drop a biscuit onto his dog bed, before zipping my key into my pocket and making my way outside.

Once on Goodie, my eyes drift across the street, taking

in the quiet row of houses, all nearly identical in style, shape, and size. Red's house is the only one in the line that looks different: it's brown instead of white and boxier than the others, with a sloped roof instead of the more traditional steeple. I notice that Grandma Jane's car is parked in Red's driveway, a sign that things between them have become even more serious since the summer. It's silly, but I always feel safer knowing that Grandma Jane is close by. Tonight, she's coming over for family dinner, and my whole body warms just thinking about it, my muscles finally relaxing after my scare upstairs.

"Sup, Parker."

I turn on my heels, coming face-to-face with Mike. I can't see his eyes because his Yankees hat is pulled down even lower than usual, so in a playful motion, I swipe it from his head.

"Give it back," he grunts with a cold edge to his voice that causes me to drop the hat in his hands. Grumbling, he tugs it back onto his head.

I stare at him for a moment. He bobs up and down and shakes out his arms as I remain still.

"What's with you?" I finally ask.

"Nothing."

I shake my head. "You're lying. Just tell me." I lower my voice even though we're alone on the street. "Is it the nightmares? Did you have another one last night?"

At this, Mike stops jumping in place, his whole body stiffening as he presses his lips together. "Something like that."

"It's OK," I urge him. "You can tell me. Was it the Oldies again?"

He goes still. "I sometimes see them burning. At night. Except in my dream, Bea is in my room, and she reaches for my throat . . ." He trails off, clearing his throat.

"Mike, I—"

He shakes his head. "Never mind. I don't want to talk about it. Let's just run, Parker. I'm fine."

"But I—"

Mike takes off running before I can finish my sentence, leaving me with no choice but to dart off after him.

"Hey," I call, catching up to his side.

"I don't want to talk about it," he tells me, keeping his eyes straight ahead.

I shrug as we run. "Fine. Whatever you want."

For a while, we move together in silence, focusing on our steps and our breaths. Just as we hit the mile mark, Mike suddenly starts slowing down. I match his pace and we continue to glide for another half a mile, when Mike screeches to a stop. He puts his hands on his hips and shakes his head.

"I can't," he says with his head down, not meeting my eyes. "I'm just too tired. I won't make it through practice if we finish this run."

I nod, catching my own breath as we walk around the stone elementary school. The colorful playground is covered in crows, a collection of sharp beaks and pointy wings. Someone probably just left food out, but it almost looks as if the birds are having some kind of secret meeting, with the biggest crow of all leading the pack from his perch on the top of the slide. I can't help but think of the bird-shaped shadows in my room.

Mike follows my gaze. "A murder," he says.

"What? Who got murdered?"

Mike laughs, the tension breaking with the sound. "No one," he says to my relief. "A group of crows is called a murder."

I blink. "Why?"

"Superstition. People used to think that black birds could predict death, and a group of crows could even *bring* death."

"That's ridiculous."

Mike looks at me, amused. "I thought superstitions like that were right up your ally, Parker."

"I don't believe in superstitions," I argue. "I believe in the paranormal—there's a difference."

Mike rolls his eyes. "If you say so."

The leader crow calls out to his friends, as if addressing them at the end of a speech. They all caw back.

"Poor crows," I say. "They don't seem unlucky."

"That's because they're not. They just have a bad rep."

We continue to watch the birds until Mike lets out a large sigh. "Let's go," he coaxes, and together we start off down the road, walking side by side.

"I'm sorry," he says after a moment, his voice tight. "I'm not trying to be a jerk lately. I'm just tired."

I meet his eyes, which are defined by dark circles and swollen lids. "I used to have nightmares," I admit quietly. "You know, after my dad died."

Sympathy colors Mike's face as he digests my words. "You did?"

I nod. "For a while, every night—no matter what I did—I had these horrible dreams. It got so bad that I was afraid to go to sleep." I shiver with the memory and cross my arms over my chest as we walk.

"Do you still get them?"

"Not really."

"What did you do to stop them?"

"I started to call my Grandma Jane."

Mike makes a face. "That's it? You just called your grandma, and the nightmares magically stopped?"

"I know it sounds dumb, but yeah, it worked. I'd call her in the middle of the night, and she'd tell me about her day, and her voice was always sweet and soothing like a cup of warm milk, and it was enough to put me to sleep. I still call her sometimes in the middle of the night—even without a nightmare." I look at him seriously. "You should call me if you have another one."

Mike snorts. "Not a chance, Parker. It'd be like two in the morning, or something."

"I don't care. Just call me. If I can't talk, I won't answer." I shrug to show how simple it all is.

"I'd feel bad if I woke you up."

"So text me. If I'm awake, I'll call you back."

Mike appears to be wavering. Finally, he nods. "Thanks, Parker." He smiles. "You're a pretty good Robin."

At this, I laugh. "You wish."

Mike's entire face is instantly lighter, his eyes and smile brightening. He stays this way until we get home, and the smile sticks during our walk to school, right up until we separate for our lockers.

"Later, Parker," he says, before disappearing down the hall.

To my surprise, Lex isn't hovering by my locker the way she has been doing every other morning. I do a quick scan of the hallways, half-expecting to see her colorful figure barreling forward, but she's nowhere in sight. So I make my way to homeroom.

She's not there either.

Is she sick? I wonder when the bell rings and she still hasn't shown up. She doesn't come to homeroom at all.

"You see Lex?" I ask Zoe afterward when we meet up in the hallway.

"Nope. She must be staying home today. We can text her at lunch."

A worried feeling gnaws at me, but I force myself to shrug it off and follow Zoe to first period.

Class keeps me so preoccupied that I don't give Lex another thought until lunch, when I'm shocked to see her sitting in her regular seat, nibbling on a turkey-and-cheese sandwich as if she's been in school all day. Just like yesterday, she's wearing all white.

"Did you just get here?" I ask, dropping my lunch bag onto the table.

Zoe and Kaylee pull up seats beside us, digging into their own lunches.

Lex smiles coyly and nods. "I needed my beauty sleep. I had a long night."

"Doing what?" Zoe asks, making a face. "We haven't really gotten any homework yet. The teachers are still being nice."

At this, Lex's eyes seem to sparkle. "I was at Abigail's."

Her words knock the wind out of me. "You were at Abigail's?" I ask. "On my street?"

She nods cheerfully. "We've got this huge project—some mansion in Westport. It's epic."

"Didn't you *just* start working there?" Kaylee asks.

"Yup. This week."

Zoe swipes a cookie from Kaylee's bag and takes a huge

bite while studying Lex. "Did your mom ground you for staying out so late?"

Lex shrugs. "She didn't even notice. She was at the high school with Carlos and Julian until forever. By the time I snuck back in, she was dead asleep."

"What about your dad?" I ask.

"Business trip," Lex says, looking almost proud of herself for being sneaky.

Zoe narrows her eyes. "So why do they have you working late? Isn't that, like, child labor? You're not even a real employee."

Kaylee and I stifle laughs at Zoe's bluntness. Lex bristles.

"I *am* a real employee. I'm their volunteer."

"But what do you *do*?" Zoe presses.

Lex sits up taller in her seat. "Lots of things."

"Like what?"

I pick at my cheese-and-pickle sandwich, barely eating as I listen.

Lex begins to list tasks: "Answer the phone, help Abigail organize her samples . . ."

"Make photocopies . . ." Zoe adds.

"Only once!" Lex insists. She sighs heavily. "You guys are the worst."

"Yeah," I chime in, "leave her alone. It's legit."

"Thank you, Quinn," Lex says, her features relaxing. "Good to know that *someone* here has my back."

Once I see that Lex has calmed down a bit, I ask, "So, how is Abigail? What's she like?"

Lex's face lights up. "She's amazing. Seriously, I've never met a cooler woman. She's got a massive walk-in closet full of designer shoes, and she let me try a pair on as we worked."

"What does a woman from South Haven need with a bunch of designer shoes?" Zoe asks. "It's not like this town is fancy or anything."

"Well, maybe she's trying to change that," Lex answers, the loyalty to her new boss becoming more and more transparent.

I take a bite of my sandwich, my next question screaming inside me. I lean forward. "What's everyone else like?"

At this, Lex's expression darkens. "They're OK," she says unconvincingly. "I mean, I'm sure I just have to win them over."

"Do they talk to you?"

She shrugs one shoulder. "Kind of."

"What about Cami? What's she like?"

"Jeez, Quinn," Zoe says. "What's with the twenty questions?"

I ignore Zoe and continue pressing Lex to answer. "Does Cami talk to you?"

"No," Lex says just as the bell begins to ring. "She hasn't said two words to me. She just kind of stares."

"She stares at you?" Kaylee balks. "Creepy."

Lex nods. "They all do. But like I said," she adds quickly, "it's just a matter of time before I win them over. You'll see."

She gathers her stuff and stands. "See you guys later," she says, walking away before I can say anything else.

Defeated, I pack up what's left of my lunch and shuffle off to class.

Lex's words follow me to practice, where instead of thinking about the drill sequence or run times, I'm picturing Cami standing in the middle of the street, her eyes narrowed in what looks like anger, or maybe jealousy.

No matter how hard I try, I can't seem to shake the feeling that something is wrong. The feeling crawls into my muscles, settling into my feet like rocks. I'm slow. Like really slow, and Coach notices.

"Pick it *up*, Parker!"

But I can't pick it up, and Jess skates past me as if she's on wheels.

"What was with you, Parker?" Mike asks me after practice, as we walk together up the hill.

"I just wasn't feeling it today," I mutter, kicking a rock between my feet.

"Is it Lex?" he asks. "What's up with her lately? Why's she wearing white? And what's she doing with the neighbors? Last night, I saw her leaving Abigail's house really late."

"She's their volunteer, remember?" I answer shortly, punting the rock into the street.

Mike makes a face. "That's still weird."

"You don't think anything's weird," I grumble. "You believe that everything can be explained with science."

He shakes his head. "Not this. This is just weird."

I study him from the corner of my eye. "Michael Warren, are you already giving up our bet?"

"What? No—never. I'm just being observant, is all."

"Uh-huh . . ."

"No way. I don't think those ladies are ghosts." He shudders. "At least, they better not be. One monster encounter was enough for a lifetime, thank you very much."

I look at him and feel myself softening. Maybe his refusal to believe in ghosts is more about fear than science. I decide to change the subject. For the rest of the walk, we talk about Mrs. Carey's latest project, and whether or not Rocky Hill will ever get bacon grilled cheese sandwiches in the cafeteria. By the time we turn onto Goodie Lane, I can tell that we're both feeling better.

"So, where are they?" Mike asks, his eyes scanning our street. "I rarely see them out here. Not like the Oldies."

"No, they're basically the opposite of the Oldies."

Mike raises an eyebrow. "You can't possibly know their routine already, Parker."

"I'm starting to. The Oldies were up early and in bed

early. But the Ladies," I nod to our new neighbors' houses, "they're usually up late. Well, except for that morning when they introduced themselves to us. I don't think that's their usual routine, though." I take a step closer to Mike, swinging my arms innocently as we walk. "You know, we *could* make it more official," I tell him, keeping my voice even. "We could start casing them for real—a little research, a little spying. Just like old times."

He snorts. "Old times without the Oldies?"

I look at him. "You have to admit: we're pretty awesome detectives."

Mike bites his bottom lip. "I can't argue with that."

"So, you in? Are we going to start investigating?"

Mike exhales loudly before flashing me a smirk. "I'm in, Parker. If, for nothing else, to see you go down on that track field after you lose our bet."

"Whatever. I already have the most amazing costume picked out for you."

"Well, I'm glad you like it, because the only place you're going to see it is on your own body this Halloween."

"Very funny."

"I *am* funny, aren't I? And you want to know what else I am?"

"Hungry?" I guess.

He laughs. "You know me too well, Parker. I'll see you tomorrow."

"Bye, Mike."

"Later."

I stand in the street as he walks away, giving me one last wave before he heads into the house. My legs are tired and want desperately to lie down on the couch inside, but they won't seem to move from off the pavement. I squint at Abigail's window, wondering if Lex is inside.

Billy yelps at the base of our living room window, breaking my trance. Just as I turn around, I spot Uncle Jack's truck easing down the street. His large arm sticks out of the open window, waving wildly at me. He beeps the horn.

"Quinnie!"

"Hey, Uncle Jack," I say as he pulls up next to me.

"What's shaking, kid?"

"Not much. What are you doing?"

"Just checking on my favorite niece." He turns off the truck and hops out, giving me one of his giant bear hugs.

"You want to stay for dinner? Grandma Jane is cooking in like an hour."

At this, Uncle Jack's eyes light up. "Janie's cooking? Well, I was just stopping by to say hi, but it looks like I'll have to swing back around. What's she making?"

"I think short ribs."

"Now you're speaking my *language*, Quinn." He all but licks his lips before stopping short as a door opens across the street. Both of our eyes follow the sound and watch Abigail as she steps onto her porch.

"Who. Is. That?" Uncle Jack breathes, lowering his aviators to get a better look.

Abigail looks as stunning as ever, wearing a short white dress and heels, her white-blonde hair pulled back into a tight ballerina bun, with a pop of red on her lips. She smiles and waves to us; I hold my breath as she begins to walk over.

"She's the new neighbor," I explain through tight lips. "Her name's Abigail."

Uncle Jack smooths out his short hair that never seems to move, and he stands up straighter, pulling his shoulders back. "How do I look?" he whispers to me.

I make a face. "Like you always do."

"Hello, there!" Abigail calls, her voice oozing an artificial sweetness that makes me roll my eyes. I look at Uncle Jack, half-expecting him to roll his eyes, too, but instead he puffs out his chest and waves. I frown as she crosses the street toward us.

"Afternoon," he tells her. "You the new neighbor?"

"Yes, I'm Abigail," she says with a smile. "And you are?"

"I'm Jack. Quinn's uncle."

Abigail's eyes widen as she looks at me, her gold locket catching the sun. "Quinn, you never told me you had an uncle."

"Why would I?" I ask.

Uncle Jack rests his heavy arm around my shoulder, squeezing a little too tightly as he expels a fake laugh. "She's such a kidder, isn't she?"

"We're not really related," I continue. "He was friends with my dad."

"Isn't that sweet?" Abigail purrs. She takes a step closer to us in a way that makes me want to take a step back.

"I try," Uncle Jack says with a smile.

"I've got homework," I mutter, wiggling out from under his grasp. "See you later, Uncle Jack."

"See you, kid."

"Goodbye, Quinn."

Without answering, I trot up the front steps and disappear inside, surprised to see Billy already hovering at the door.

"Hey, boy," I say, ruffling his fur. His eyes remain focused on the door, a small, low growl building in the back of his throat. "What's wrong?"

As if in response, Billy jumps onto the couch by the living room window and stares out at the street with his tail wagging.

"That's just Uncle Jack," I say, plopping down on the couch beside him. But then I follow his gaze, and see that Abigail is still in my driveway, flirting with my uncle right in broad daylight. I can hear Uncle Jack's laughter from inside.

"Come on, Billy," I say. "This is making me kind of sick."

Together, we disappear into the kitchen, where I remain with my homework until Grandma Jane and Red arrive with the groceries for dinner.

"Step aside, step aside! Hot stuff coming through!" Grandma Jane calls, her voice rising up from behind a giant Crock-Pot.

"Hot stuff is right," Red jokes, his eyes twinkling. "And she's not just talking about the short ribs."

"Red, you flirt! Now get over here and help me. Frances will be here any minute."

I set the table as Grandma Jane and Red bustle around the small kitchen, reheating meats and vegetables, browning homemade dinner buns. Grandma has lit some candles and switched on Mom's small radio, swaying her hips in a flurry of crystals and beads. By the time Mom rolls in, everything's ready to serve.

"This looks delicious, Jane," Mom says, taking her seat at the head of the table. "Should we dig in?"

"Not without me, you shouldn't!" a booming voice calls from the foyer.

Amused, Mom twitches her eyebrow. "Jack," she says simply. "I should have known that you'd smell the food."

"Good Lord, this looks good," Uncle Jack says, pulling up a chair next to me. "Janie, when are you going to ditch

Red over there and marry me instead? I'd let you cook for me every day of the week."

"What a treat for me," Grandma says dryly, plating up a heaping serving of ribs for Jack to pass down.

"I *am* a treat," Uncle Jack insists, sampling a rib from off the plate he's supposed to be passing. Grandma Jane slaps his hand, forcing him to pass it down to me.

"You owe me a rib," I tell him, shooting him a look.

Uncle Jack drops his half-eaten rib onto my plate. "Here you go," he says with a wink. "Don't say I never gave you anything."

"Eww, gross!"

Grandma Jane shakes her head. "Seriously, Jack? If you keep this up, then you don't get any dessert."

"Aww, don't tease me like that, Janie. I'm celebrating!"

"What are you celebrating?" Mom asks. "You eat the most chicken wings at work again?"

"That was one time, Frances. And it was your husband's idea."

"It may have been his idea, but you certainly didn't need any arm twisting . . .'"

"Oh, enough, you two," Grandma says. She smiles at me. "Do you have enough to eat, dear?"

I nod, my mouth full of the sweet and spicy ribs, with meat so tender that it falls off the bone. "Perfect," I say after a big swallow. "Thanks, Grandma."

She beams at me. "Anything for my special girl."

Uncle Jack clears his throat loudly, and Grandma Jane sighs. "Do you have something to say, Jack?"

He pretends to look coy. "Just waiting patiently for someone to ask me why I'm in such a good mood."

"The ribs, right?" I ask. "Don't you always celebrate when we have ribs?"

"No, no, Quinnie. This is bigger than the ribs. This is about a woman."

I freeze as I realize what he's about to say.

"Really?" Mom asks. "Who?"

"Your neighbor."

"*My* neighbor?"

"Yeah. You know, the one who just moved in across the street. Abigail."

"You actually asked her out?" Grandma Jane presses. "And she said *yes*?"

"Of course she said yes."

I stare at him, horrified. "Are you really going out with her? Just the two of you—like, *alone*?"

"That's usually how dates work, kiddo."

"But don't you think she's kind of . . ." I trail off, unsure of how to word what I want to say.

Mom leans across the table, pointing her fork at Uncle Jack. "Do *not*, under any circumstance, take her to the tavern for dinner."

Uncle Jack blinks. "What's wrong with the tavern? James used to love it there."

"No, Frances is right," Grandma Jane agrees. "The tavern is definitely not first-date material, dear."

My stomach turns, and I can't eat any more of these ribs. "But don't you think . . ." Once again, I trail off, my skin burning up as the four faces stare at me across the table. I sigh. "Never mind."

Uncle Jack pats me on the back with his heavy hand. "Cheer up, kiddo. Even if things with Abigail get serious, you'll still see me around. Heck, I'll just bring her with me next time Janie cooks."

"Oh, please do," Mom says with a smirk.

"Yes, the more the merrier," Grandma Jane adds. "You know me—I cook for an army anyway. Although something tells me that Abigail doesn't eat all that much. I've only seen her in passing, but she's built like a bird. Have you met her yet, Frances?"

Mom shakes her head. "No. I had to work during the open house, and we just don't seem to be on the same schedule. Quinn's met her, though, haven't you, sweetie?"

My body stiffens as I nod. "Yes, I've met her."

Before I can elaborate, Uncle Jack smacks his lips together loudly. "I'm telling you, Janie, you've outdone yourself yet again. I'm willing to give up my date with Abigail to have dinner with you instead. Interested?"

"Oh, Jack. You sure know how to flatter a woman," Grandma Jane says, exchanging an eye roll with Mom.

"Heaven," Jack continues, closing his eyes. "Absolute heaven."

The conversation soon shifts to other, more mundane things: school, work, the traffic that Mom has to fight every day to get to the hospital, the construction on the parkway, the fall allergies that Red is currently suffering from. I sit through it all with my mind across the street. First Lex, now Uncle Jack. Something doesn't seem right, but I'm not quite sure what.

Once we're finished eating, we clean the dishes together and we sing along to Grandma's Motown playlist, and with the setting of the sun, our guests make their goodbyes. Uncle Jack is the first to barrel down the front steps, followed by Red. Grandma Jane hangs back and pulls gently on my arm.

"Take this," she whispers, holding out a green crystal the size of my palm. "Keep it with you."

"What is it?" I ask.

"Just a bit of extra protection. It might help you sleep better." She closes my fingers around it and squeezes.

If there was ever a time for me to voice my concerns about the Ladies in White, this is that moment. But before I can find my words, Red loops an arm around my grandma's shoulders, and her face lights up under his warmth.

"Shall we, my dear?"

"We shall," she tells him.

She looks so happy, and I lose my nerve. "Goodnight, Grandma Jane," I say, tucking the crystal into my pocket. "Night, Red."

I watch from the doorway as they bound forward into the dark. The crystal feels heavy in my jeans, as if it's weighing me down.

"Don't forget it's garbage night," Mom reminds me from the kitchen, giving a pointed look toward the bag brimming with the remnants of dinner.

I sigh and gather up the trash, dumping it into the bin outside. I then tilt back the barrel and drag it to the curb. As I set it down onto the concrete, I notice a light flickering across the street at Abigail's house. The front door opens, and out pops Lex.

"Thank you so much, Abigail. I'll see you tomorrow after school," she says.

I watch as my friend descends the porch steps, her gaze still focused on her boss even as Mrs. Vega's sedan pulls into Abigail's driveway. Lex climbs into her mother's car, and she seems to notice me only as they begin to drive away. Her eyes widen.

Mrs. Vega rolls down her window and smiles. "Hi, Quinn. How you doing, honey?"

"I'm good, Mrs. Vega. Hi, Lex."

Lex waves. "Hey, Quinn."

"Say hello to your mom for me," Mrs. Vega says, waggling her fingers in the air. "Tell her we need a lunch date one of these days if she's not working."

"Will do. Have a good night."

My stomach tenses as I watch them drive away. When I turn back around, I notice that Abigail is still standing in her doorframe, watching with a tight scowl as Mrs. Vega and Lex disappear. Once they're out of sight, she sharply turns and goes inside, shutting her door without so much as a *hello* or *goodbye* to me.

Billy scratches on the door behind me, startling me back to attention. I finish positioning the garbage bin and head back to my own house. As I reach the top step, I suddenly feel a presence, as if someone is watching me. Spinning around, I don't see anything—nobody's there, and all four houses across the street are quiet. My eyes focus on Cami's house on the end. It's almost as if I can see her dark brown eyes looking out at me through the top window, but when I blink, I see nothing. Shaking it off, I head inside.

Later I dream about running. I'm wearing my favorite red shorts with the white piping along the bottoms, and my lucky red-striped tank top—the same one I was wearing when Mike and I defeated the Oldies on the Fourth of July. I'm holding a baton in my right hand—the kind that we use in track meets, only I'm not at a track meet; I'm by the pond. I'm looking for someone. Or something. I'm out of breath and sweating, and the darkness is closing in around me. I run faster, but every time I try to get away from the pond, I end up just circling back to the lightning tree. It reaches out to me with its long, crooked limbs. Then, all of a sudden, a white mist rises from the water, and I get very, very cold—so cold that I drop the baton. I'm about to scream, when a phone rings.

Wait—what?

The ringing becomes louder and more persistent. I stare across the pond, trying to pinpoint where the noise is coming from.

Open your eyes, a voice tells me.

I listen, jolting up in bed, suddenly awake and lucid as my phone buzzes on the bedside table, softly humming the *Batman* theme song. Mike.

"Hello?" I whisper.

"Hey," he whispers back.

I let my head fall against my headboard as I try to adjust my eyes to the dark. "You OK?"

"No."

I nod even though he can't see me. Goosebumps line my arm just like they did in my dream. It makes me want to know what Mike's nightmare was about: What was it that scared him so much? Was it the Oldies? Or did he see the pond like I did?

I consider asking him, but maybe he won't want to talk about it—maybe I don't want to really talk about it. My mind flutters through different subjects, trying to think of something to say. In this moment, Billy pushes his way into the room, as if to check in on me. I lean over and pat the end of my bed, and he jumps up, before rolling into a crescent shape by my feet.

"Did I ever tell you about the day we got Billy?" I ask into the phone.

"No," Mike answers, his voice lightening. "I just assumed you adopted him as a puppy."

"Not exactly." I settle back against my pillow, pressing Grandma Jane's green crystal into my palm. "I was four. Dad was working late. I remember waiting at the window for him to come home. When he finally did, he was all excited about something. 'Come on,' he told Mom and me. 'I have a surprise for you.' I remember Mom worrying about dinner getting cold, but Dad just kept on smiling, leading us out the door."

"Was Billy in the driveway or something?" Mike asks.

"Nope. We got in the car, and Dad gave me a lollipop—"

"What flavor?"

I blink. "Does it matter?"

"Of course it matters," Mike insists, his voice suddenly animated. "If it was something gross like root beer, then I will question your accuracy as a storyteller."

"Fine, OK, the lollipop was strawberry. Happy? And at any rate, I happen to like root beer."

"It tastes like medicine."

"You're so wrong."

"No, really. It's got this chemical in it—methyl salicylate—which is actually a poison. They say that the amount found in root beer is harmless. Still, it's strong enough to make most other cultures spit it out—"

"Mike!"

"Oh, sorry." He laughs slightly across the line. "Continue."

"Anyway," I say, "we drove through town until we got to the South Haven woods. 'Oh good, he's still here,' Dad said. Mom and I asked him who he was talking about, and that was the first time I noticed the dog treats sitting next to my car seat. When Dad got me out of the car, he set me down on the grass and—"

"There was Billy?"

I smile. "There was Billy."

"What was he doing in the woods?"

"We don't know. Dad found him while he was on patrol. Billy liked him immediately, but he was too scared to get in the car. That's why Dad left to get the dog treats, and he picked us up on the way back. I heard him tell Mom that he put in calls to all of the local shelters, but no one claimed him."

"Did Billy jump right in the car when he saw the treats?"

"Mom got him in. And then he came home with us, and the rest is history." I ruffle the fur on Billy's back, remembering the way he used to follow Dad all around the house, and how I used to drop Goldfish on the floor, trying to make him like me best. It never worked, though. Dad was always his favorite.

Mike yawns loudly across the other end and mumbles something that I can't quite make out.

"You still there?" I ask.

I listen for a moment and am answered by a heavy silence, then the sound of slow, even breaths. Mike's fallen asleep.

"Sweet dreams," I whisper, before hanging up the phone.

CHAPTER 7

Talking to Mike on the phone must have done the trick last night, because he slept through our run the following morning.

"What happened to you?" I demand when he emerges for our walk to school. "I waited for over ten minutes. You didn't even text."

"I overslept," he mumbles, shuffling his feet beside me as though he's still half-dreaming.

At this, I smile. "The Billy story worked?"

He laughs. "Maybe a little bit."

"No nightmares?"

"Not after I called you."

To avoid letting him see me blush, I step ahead. "You'd better pick up the pace now, or else we'll be late. Come on, sleepyhead."

Together, we lengthen our strides and move in a quick rhythm along the sidewalk, past the succession of cars heading downtown. By the time we reach Rocky Hill, Mike already seems exhausted.

"Looks like you could use a few more stories this week," I tell him.

On cue, he yawns. "I just need to catch up," he tells me. "Couple more days of some solid sleep, and I'll be back to normal." He points down the hallway. "I'm going to go put my head down in homeroom. See you at practice, Parker." He starts to walk off but then suddenly turns back around, his face close to mine. "By the way, thanks for last night." He smiles, and it's the most genuine and grateful expression that I've ever seen him make. My knees buckle under the warmth of it.

"Any time," I tell him, and I mean it.

Once again, he turns to walk away, only this time, Zoe jumps in my face.

"Hey, Quinnie."

"Morning," I tell her. She loops her arm through mine and steers me toward my locker, where Lex is waiting. I nearly drop my books at the sight of her. She's hovering silently with a spaced-out look on her face, and she looks paler than usual.

"Hey, Lex."

She doesn't answer. Her eyes remain focused on the

pile of binders clutched between her arms. I wave a hand in front of her.

"Hel-lo?"

She blinks and sets her widened eyes on me, as if noticing me for the first time. "Oh. Good morning, Quinn. Hi, Zoe."

"Are you OK?" I ask, reaching out to touch her arm. It's cold to the touch, and I quickly pull back. "Do you want us to bring you to the nurse? Or call your mom to come get you?"

"Why would I need that? I'm fine."

And without another word, she wanders off to homeroom, not even bothering to wait for me.

Zoe and I exchange looks. "Somebody needs to get to bed earlier," she mutters.

I clutch my binders to my chest and don't answer.

Things don't get any less strange at lunch, when Lex barely speaks or eats.

"I'm seriously getting worried about you," I tell her, nudging her with an Oreo. "At least eat this if you don't want your sandwich."

Lex shrugs off the cookie. "I'm fine, Quinnie. Just tired."

My body stiffens. "Did you have another late night at Abigail's?"

At the mere mention of Abigail's name, Lex perks up, the color suddenly filling her cheeks so that she looks almost healthy again. "Yeah, Abigail picked up another big client, and the deadline is kind of killing everyone."

"Why do you have to stay so late?" Kaylee asks, narrowing her eyes. "I mean, you're just a volunteer."

"We need all hands on deck," she says, sitting up a little straighter. "And Abigail says that I'm mature for my age."

At this, Zoe laughs so hard that she spits out her water. "You? Mature?" She laughs again.

Lex scowls at her. "Besides, Abigail didn't *keep* me. I wanted to stay."

"But that's even more weird!"

"It's not weird!" Lex stomps to her feet and gathers her unopened lunchbox.

"Where are you going?" we all ask at once.

"Anywhere but here," Lex mutters, before storming out of the cafeteria.

"Whoa," Zoe breathes.

I toss my Oreo at her. "That was totally your fault."

"What?" she asks innocently. "I was just saying what you were both thinking."

"I'll go see if she's OK," Kaylee says, managing to slip out of the cafeteria without the teacher on duty noticing.

Zoe takes a bite out of my Oreo. She rolls her eyes at me. "What?"

"I'm worried about her," I admit, my shoulders slumping.

"Yeah," Zoe sighs, putting down the rest of the cookie. "Me too."

Together, we stare after the cafeteria door, as if willing our friend to find her way back to us.

I don't see Lex again until after school. She approaches my locker with a cautious look on her face, as if she's nervous to talk to me after what happened in the cafeteria.

I smile at her, trying to set her at ease. "Hey, Lex."

"Hey," she says back. "You have practice now?"

I sling my backpack over my shoulder. "Yup."

"Cool. I'll probably see you on your street later."

"What?" I ask, and then I immediately feel silly because I know. "Oh, for Abigail?"

She nods. "We've got to finish this big project before the weekend. It's probably going to be another late night."

I slam my locker door closed a little too hard before turning to Lex. "You know you don't have to stay the whole time, right? I mean, you probably *shouldn't* stay the whole time. It's . . ."

She bats her long lashes. "It's *amazing*. It's exciting. It's everything I'd ever dreamed about."

"It's weird," I say before I can stop myself.

Her face immediately clouds over. "Not you too, Quinn. Zoe was bad enough at lunch."

"I'm sorry," I tell her, "but you have to admit, it's kind of strange that Abigail would keep a kid working so late."

"I told you. She thinks I'm mature."

"Yeah, but you're not." *Oh no.* My muscles tighten. *Now I've done it.*

Lex crosses her arms over her chest and glares at me. "Sorry for trying something new."

"Hey, I didn't mean anything by it . . ." I trail off as she waves her hand at me.

"Whatever, Quinn. I've always supported you and Kaylee with your running. And Zoe with her piano stuff."

"It's not that I don't support you—"

"Well, it sure feels that way." With this, she stomps off in the opposite direction.

"Lex, wait!"

But she doesn't wait. She doesn't even turn around. My stomach sinks as I watch her disappear. *Good going, Quinn.* I need to text Zoe and let her know that Lex is mad at me, but when I pull out my phone, the time sends a jolt up my spine. I'm late for practice! And it was my turn to lead warm-ups.

I bolt toward the gym with my backpack bouncing behind me, not stopping until I reach the exit to the field. Then I run down the hill toward the field house, where I change as fast as humanely possible.

By the time I make it to the track, Jess is already leading the warm-ups alongside the boys' captain, Shreyas. I drop my bag onto the water bench and join in the back next to Mike, who flashes me a worried look.

You OK? he mouths. I nod and throw myself into the warm-ups.

When we're done, Coach blows his whistle for us to start drills. As we break off into different directions, Jess bumps me with her shoulder. Hard.

"Hey!" I cry, rubbing my arm. She ignores me and keeps walking. "Rude, much?" I mumble.

She hears and spins around, marching back toward me. "*I'm* rude? At least I didn't skip the warm-up."

"I'm sorry," I say. Although I don't feel sorry. With everything going on with Lex and the neighbors, the last thing I need is Jess giving me a hard time on the field. "It's not even a big deal."

At this, her eyes widen. "Not a big deal? Well if it's not important to you, then maybe you shouldn't be captain."

"Oh, calm down, Jess. It was *one* time."

"One time too many!"

I take a breath to compose myself before squaring my shoulders off against her. My dad taught me how to run. I've been doing it my entire life. I've made friends on this team, I've given every morning, afternoon, and weekend—rain or shine. Running is who I am. No one is going to take it away from me—not the Oldies, not the Ladies in White, and especially not Jessica Zagha.

"Face it, Quinn," she continues. "You're not cut out to lead."

"Me?" My body warms as I launch forward, my fists balled at my sides. "You're taking practice way too seriously, and the team hates it. You act like you're the coach. Look at your stupid little whistle." I flick the plastic whistle around her neck and watch Jess visibly tense up.

A crowd has gathered, but I don't care. It's like all of the tension that I've been feeling in my stomach is suddenly rising up, taking aim at the target in front of me. I lose all sense of control. "No one likes you," I yell. "No one ever has!"

Hurt colors her face, but she folds her arms across her chest and raises her voice to match mine. "At least I care about this team. You only care about one thing: Mike *Warren*." She throws a sneer toward a sheepish-looking Mike just as Coach calls our names from across the field.

Jess and I take another step toward each other and are huffing and puffing, nose to nose. All of our teammates are surrounding us, waiting on our next words. Jess looks as if she's about to really let loose on me, but suddenly Coach is at our side, blowing his whistle in between us.

"Enough!" he cries, causing me to fall back and shake my head at the ringing in my ears. "Tenley and Maya—you run the drills. Everyone, line up!"

I start to follow my team when Coach pulls Jess and me back. "Everyone except you two. You're benched for today, *and* for Saturday's meet. Now go sit down."

"But Coach, I—" Jess starts.

"Save it!"

"But we're—" I try.

"I said save it! Go sit on that bench and think about what it means to be leaders. I chose you to set an example, not fight. You let me down today." His face falls from anger to disappointment in one breath, and without another word, he stalks off toward our replacements and the rest of the team.

Jess and I fall against the bench, defeated in every sense of the word.

The rest of practice is brutal, just sitting and watching and feeling everyone's gaze on us. When Coach blows his whistle, Jess bolts from the bench, disappearing into the field house. I wait until most of my teammates have cleared off before I grab my bag and pull myself to my feet.

Mike is waiting for me at the bottom of the hill, like always. He presses his lips together and gives a small wave. His expression looks full of pity; it stops me in my tracks, the heat rising to my cheeks. There's no way that I can face him right now.

Without a word, I turn on my heels and bolt in the opposite direction, through the back exit of the field. I can hear Mike calling after me, but I just run faster—through the fence, through the trees, until I land on the street behind the school. The pavement twists and turns beneath my sneakers as I snake up and down the side streets. I'm crying and sweating, but I don't stop, not until I reach my destination: Unity Cemetery.

My legs seize up as soon as I approach the black iron gate. I haven't been here since May, since the one-year anniversary of Dad's death. Mom and I came together, each of us wearing one of Dad's old T-shirts. We brought bottles of homemade iced tea and chocolate glazed donuts from the bakery—the kind Dad always used to buy me. Except I couldn't eat or drink a thing, so Mom just held me as I cried. Mom continues to visit, but every time she's asked if I want to join, I've made excuses so that I haven't had to come back. She told me that when I'm ready, Dad will be there. Truth is, I don't like seeing my dad this way: as just a stone marker in the ground.

I wonder if it was a mistake to come here by myself. My fingers clench the gate as I rock back and forth on my heels. But I've already come this far. There's no turning back now. Besides, I'm not ready to talk to Mike yet—that's probably him making my phone buzz in my pocket. The only one I want to talk to is Dad. So after a deep breath, I push forward.

The grass looks freshly trimmed along the hilly paths, and the air smells like burning leaves. Even though I've only been here a few times, my muscles remember the way, moving on autopilot until I reach the giant oak tree; to the left of it is Dad's headstone.

Fresh flowers are bundled at the base (probably from Mom), along with a smooth black crystal (probably from Grandma Jane). Beside them waves a tiny flag with the police academy's logo. Uncle Jack must have left it. It's oddly comforting to know that he still visits. I think he cried harder than I did at the funeral.

I fall to my knees on the grass and run my shaking fingers over Dad's name etched in stone. I wonder what Mom does when she's here. Does she talk out loud? Tell him about her day? Or about me?

"Hi," I say, my voice ragged. The wind is gentle through my hair. For some reason, I take this as a sign to keep going. "I—I'm sorry for not coming here that much..." I trail off, feeling stupid. The quiet seeps in around me, filling the space with a calm that gives me the courage to keep going.

"I just . . ." The tears start to well up again. "I had a bad day. I was worried about Lex, and I took it out on one of my teammates and now—" I sniffle. "And now I'm benched for the next meet."

Saying it out loud makes me feel so sick that I have to brace myself against the stone. It's cool against my forehead, and I stay this way until the wave of dizziness passes.

"I messed up, Dad," I continue. "And I don't know how to fix it. Running is everything to me and now ..." I keep losing my words, not sure how to say what I really feel. "I miss you."

The breeze swirls around me, grazing my cheek with its warmth. I close my eyes and listen to the sounds of the cemetery: the leaves of the oak tree rustling above my head, and the birds having a conversation on its thick branches. By the time I reopen my eyes, I'm no longer crying. I wipe my cheeks with the back of my hand, before pulling myself to my feet.

"I'll come again soon," I promise, backing away from his stone. I know it's silly, but for a second I wait for him to answer. When he doesn't, I turn away. "Bye, Dad."

Then I'm off, wandering down the worn gravel path, my eyes flickering from stone to stone, reading the names of their owners. I can't help but wonder about them: who they were in life, what loved ones they left behind. Some plots are piled high with elaborate flower arrangements. Others look as though they've never been visited.

I'm so busy reading that I miss the turn to the gate, and when I look up, I find myself in an unfamiliar dark corner of the cemetery, an area shaded with heavy trees that block out all traces of sunlight. The warm breeze that had comforted me in Dad's spot has been replaced by a sudden burst of cold. Shivering, I spin around, looking for the path out. My eyes pause across the grounds, on a tombstone that seems spaced away from all the others. Something about it feels lonely, with the grass growing tall around it, as if the space has been forgotten by the groundskeeper. With cautious steps, I walk up the tiny hill, then gasp as I read the inscription on the stone.

ABIGAIL DROUT MCCLAIN
BELOVED WIFE AND MOTHER
1926–1957
"FOREVER—IS COMPOSED OF NOWS." —EMILY DICKINSON

Where have I seen that quote before? My memories flutter backward until it comes to me. I reach into my pocket, fumbling for my phone and googling my neighbor's name. Design on Goodie pops onto my screen.

Abigail Drout McClain . . .

Abigail Drout.

It's her! My heart beats wildly as I open my message box, swiping past the one text from Mom, the two from Zoe, the two from Kaylee, and the ten from Mike. I reply back to his last message without even reading it.

It's her! I type, before attaching a photo of the headstone.

What? he writes back instantly. **Parker where are you?**

No time to explain, I answer. **But we need to research. Tomorrow after school. You in?**

The three little dots dance across the screen until he finally types back, **I'm in. You sure you're OK?**

I'm fine, I tell him, just as the wind picks up around me. **Got to go. See you tomorrow.**

I tuck my phone back into my pocket as a shadow rises in front of me. Startled, I lay eyes on a well-dressed old woman with tumbles of silver hair. She stares at me so intensely that I shrink back.

"There you are!" another woman says, approaching from the sidewalk. Her hands are on the hips of her nursing uniform. "Gwen, what are you up to?" She notices me and smiles. "Sorry if we startled you." Without waiting for an answer, she gently takes the old woman's arm and starts to lead her away from the graveyard.

I shiver and make a run for it. With each step, I try to shake away the cold and shadows—the feeling of being watched. Abigail's headstone. The old woman's eyes.

For the first time ever, I'm grateful that Mom's working late. I'll have plenty of time alone to do a bit of research.

But when I turn down Goodie Lane, I spot Grandma Jane's car parked in the driveway. She's leaning against the back bumper, her arms folded across her chest. Our eyes meet, and she smiles.

"Hi, honey." She holds her hands out to me, her billowy sleeves flapping in the wind like two purple flags.

My stomach sinks a little as I guess why she's here. "Did Mom call you?"

She pulls away from our hug and nods. "After Coach called her." I shift my gaze to the ground, but I feel her studying me. She squeezes my hands. "You OK, pumpkin?"

I shrug one shoulder. "I'm fine."

"You want to talk about it?"

I shake my head, staring down at my shoelaces because I kind of want to cry again, thinking about being benched.

"Come now," Grandma Jane says. "Let's collect Billy and go to my house. You could use a cup of my special tea. We'll make a fresh batch together. How does that sound?"

It sounds like a relief. I don't really want to be alone anymore. I go inside and hook Billy to his leash; he looks so happy to see Grandma Jane waiting for him outside.

"Oh, there's my good boy," she tells him, bending down to ruffle his fur. He seems to smile in return. Grandma Jane then opens the back door to her car. "In you go, Billy. I've got treats for you at home." His ears perk up at the word *treats* as he hops in.

"You too," Grandma Jane tells me.

I climb into the passenger seat. She starts the car, and we cruise through town all the way to the border of South Haven, where the forest meets the sea. Grandma Jane lives in Valport, a small beach town with a fishing port and a lighthouse. She sings along to the radio as she steers us past mom-and-pop shops and restaurants, boats and buoys, and an illuminated sign that reads: **BEST FISH AND CHIPS IN CONNECTICUT!**

Grandma Jane's house is two stories tall and painted the same shade of blue as the sea. It's been that way since they moved in when my dad was a kid, apparently. We used to spend every birthday and holiday here, but I haven't been here for a few months now. It always felt kind of magical. Even to Billy, who leaps out of the car as soon as Grandma Jane opens the door—his old limbs suddenly appearing limber and strong.

Grandma Jane chuckles. "Someone's excited!"

Following them inside, I feel myself start to smile, my muscles loosening. The familiar scents of lavender and rosemary envelop me as we step into the colorful living room. Grandma Jane's decorating style is lots of deep greens and blues, antiques, candles, crystals, and herbs. Family photographs hang haphazardly in mismatched frames. Pictures of me growing up. My parents' wedding. My dad as a baby, as a kid, as a teenager, smiling wide in every shot.

Billy trots ahead of us to the kitchen. We follow. Grandma Jane tosses him a treat, and he curls up on the floor to enjoy it. She then lights a thick, jade candle, switches on the radio, and claps her hands together.

"Now. Tea time!" she sings. "Be a dear and grab the black tea leaves."

She points to the back wall of the kitchen, to rows upon rows of wooden shelves that balance glass jars of herbs and spices, a stone pestle and mortar, oils, long-stick matches, sprigs of rosemary, and Grandma's tea collection. I stand on my tiptoes and search for the leaves, which are curled up in clumps at the bottom of the largest jar. My fingers brush against the wood as I pull the jar down. Grandpa was a carpenter and made all these shelves, apparently. But like my dad, he died too young of a heart attack, and I never got to meet him.

"Did you find them?" Grandma Jane asks.

I spin around, clutching the jar against my chest. "Yup."

"Oh, lovely. Now smell this." She pulls out a cooled baking tray full of charred herbs. She picks them up, one at a time, and holds them out for me to inhale. "Mint for clarity. Rosemary for concentration. Chamomile and lavender for calming." She winks at me. "And a little dandelion for emotional cleansing." Then she hands me a kitchen knife. "Now, let's get chopping."

I breathe in the different scents as we dice up the ingredients, swaying to the music. We add everything into a bowl, then we put the tea leaves into the mixture and stir. When everything is mixed, we pack the tea in the steeper and fill up a few small jars with the extra. Grandma Jane already has the kettle on.

"Why don't you sit and enjoy a cup while I start on dinner?" I watch as she strains the herbs through the boiling water. The tea blooms in my cup. Then she dances back over to the counter, mixing ingredients in pots and pans, filling the kitchen with the most delicious smells.

I watch her as I sip my tea, feeling the soothing effects of it moving through my body, but my mind still feels restless.

I realize I haven't really had time alone with Grandma Jane for a while. I haven't really gotten to ask her much about everything that happened.

"Hey, Grandma?" I ask.

"Yes, sweetie?"

I bite my bottom lip, gathering my courage to ask her a question that's been on my mind since last summer. "I was wondering . . ."

"Yes?"

"Can you see into the future at all?" I blurt out.

Her laugh rises like a piano trill. "Goodness, no, dear. I don't have those kinds of powers."

"Then what kind of powers *do* you have?"

She shrugs one shoulder as she turns off the faucet, drying her hands on the dish towel. "No powers, really. I just know my way around herbs and crystals." She moves over to the fridge and takes out a stick of butter, setting it down on the counter. She swipes at it with a knife, dropping a chunk into the hot pan.

"But how did you know about Ms. Bea this summer?" I press.

She frowns at the name. "That wasn't magic, dear. That was just good old-fashioned *instinct*. Where did you think your father got it from? Now be a love and hand me that crushed pepper."

I let her words sink in as I hand her another jar from the shelf, and before I know it, she sweeps me up into her dance in the kitchen. We cook side by side, and by the time she drives me home, I really do feel better.

Just like magic.

CHAPTER 8

That night, I have another strange dream.

I'm alone, walking down Goodie, out toward the pond. It's still early, just before sunrise. A thick gray mist hovers along the top of the murky water, causing me to pull my hoodie down over my head. I peer out from under the soft blue fabric.

"Hello?" I call. "Is someone here?"

No answer. I continue to make my way around the embankment, my sneakers squelching in the mud.

"Quinn!" a voice calls. It sounds far away and hollow, and completely, utterly desperate. Something about it, though, sounds familiar. Almost like . . .

"Dad?"

My heart beats faster as I wait for the voice to answer me, and then all at once I hear it tunneling through the mist. "Quinn!"

"Dad!" I cry back. "I'm here!" I jerk my head from side to side, feeling my way through the darkness until I'm underneath the bones of the lightning tree. "Dad? Where are you?"

"Quinn!"

I try to run toward the direction of the voice, but it's as if my sneakers have suddenly become cemented to the ground. The pond emits a warm glow just before a skeletal hand thrusts itself through the water, digging its hard digits into the flesh of my ankle, pulling me down. I scream and kick and claw at the mud, but it's useless—the hand is too strong. Just as I think it's all over, a song rings out through the darkness, rising like the sun through the trees.

Batman.

"Mike?" I cry, throwing desperate glances from one side to the next. "Mike! I'm here—help! I'm over here!"

The song plays again, louder and louder, until it's as if the guitar is strumming those staccato notes right in my ear.

And then I realize that it *is* playing in my ear, or next to my ear. My eyes slowly open and focus on the comfort of my dim bedroom. My back is drenched with sweat. At my side, my phone buzzes out the *Batman* theme song. Sitting up, I snatch it from the nightstand.

"Mike?"

"Sorry to call so late," he whispers.

I check the time: it's eleven o'clock. "It's not so late. Besides, I was kind of already up."

"You OK?" he asks. "You sound out of breath."

"Just a bad dream," I admit, settling back down against the pillow.

"You too?"

"Yeah."

I reach over and grab Randy, the teddy bear that my dad gave me when I was three. I still keep him on my bed, even though I know that I'm too old for stuffed toys. The brown fur is matted from years of snuggles and love.

"What was your dream about?" I ask.

"I'd rather talk about something else," he says, his voice shaky. "Like, *anything* else."

"It's OK if you're still not over the Oldies," I tell him. "I don't think I'll ever be able to forget what we saw."

He doesn't answer, and it kind of makes me wish that I could hug him. Instead, I sigh into the phone. "I know you don't want to hear it, but I'm really worried about the new neighbors. I'm thinking it might be Oldies 2.0."

"Come on, Parker. What are the odds of that? Like one in twenty million."

"Still," I say, "when we first started investigating the Oldies, I always had this funny feeling in my stomach. And I have that same feeling now."

"Hypervigilance."

"No, it's not. Look, I know you're scared, but—"

"I never said I was scared!"

"It's OK, Mike. I'm scared, too. But I'm also worried about Lex. I think she's in trouble."

He breathes heavily into the phone. "What do you mean?"

"I think they're ghosts, Mike."

He doesn't answer.

"She hasn't been herself. I don't trust them."

"I don't know, Parker. They haven't given us a reason not to trust them."

I can practically hear him thinking as I tuck my phone under my chin. My feet move soundlessly across the room until I'm standing in front of my bedroom window. Cami's house is dark across the street—actually, most of their houses are dim, except for Abigail's, which is lit from every angle. Squinting, I stare at the big picture window and see all the Ladies in White there, probably working late. But I gasp when I see Lex sitting cross-legged on a white sofa. She's laughing, her head thrown back, her smile genuine—a smile that I haven't seen since she started volunteering there. Why don't we see this side of her anymore? What does Abigail offer that we don't? A heaviness sinks down into my stomach. Is it doubt? Or nerves? I'm not sure. All I know is that I need some answers. Soon.

"What are you doing at dawn?" I ask into the phone.

He snorts. "Hopefully, sleeping. Why?"

"I think we need to spy on them," I tell him. "You know, like through Bea's old window."

I hear him groan. "Why in the world would you want to do that?"

"Because Lex is there now, and I bet she'll still be there in the morning. Don't you want to see for yourself? Find out what's going on?"

"So you want to trample what's left of Bea's old rose-bushes, just to watch some normal ladies argue over paint swatches? Come on, Parker. We've got to be logical about this."

I bristle. "OK, you want to be logical? You want facts? I'll give you facts. First: it's always cold when we're around the Ladies in White. Second: at the party, Cami's hand totally turned see-through and the glass went through it. Third: they seem to have a weird hold over Lex. And fourth: *Abigail has a grave!* That's way too much evidence to ignore." I feel my heart beating faster in my chest as I plop back down onto my bed. "You can keep on denying it, but I know you, Mike Warren. You're suspicious."

"Not suspicious," he corrects. *"Curious."*

"Fine," I huff. "Stay in bed. I'll go without you."

"That's not a good idea, Parker."

"Why not? You said they're just *normal* women, right?"

"They are normal women. But that doesn't mean I think you should go spying on them." He sighs loudly into the receiver. "At least not alone."

I smile as he takes the bait. "So come with me, then."

"Fine," he says. "But not because I think you're right. Because I want to keep you out of trouble."

I'll take it. "See you at six, Robin." Then I quickly hang up before he can argue and try to convince me that he's Batman.

My body settles back against my pillow. Shapes and shadows crisscross along the ceiling, and without the warmth of Mike's voice, I feel cold again all over. The walls suddenly feel as if they're caving in on me, pressing down, burying me into my sheets. Panic flutters in my veins as I clutch Randy tighter to my chest, unable to move. *What's happening?* I want to scream but can't. Then, as if sensing something is wrong, Billy whines on the other side of my bedroom door, before pushing his nose through it. As soon as he licks my hand, I become unfrozen, the room instantly feeling warmer with his presence.

"Hey, boy," I whisper, bending down to rub his head. "You want up?" I ask. He blinks in response and nudges the blanket again. Gingerly, I lift him up and set him on the end of the bed. Within seconds, he is curled into a crescent moon, and the rhythmic sound of his snoring is enough to put me back to sleep.

I don't stir again until my alarm buzzes at six.

Billy cracks open one eye and frowns at me as if to say *Shut that darn thing off!*

"Sorry, bud." I swipe away my alarm and drag myself to the closet, where I pull on a navy blue hoodie and a pair of clean jeans; I stuff Grandma Jane's crystal into the front pocket. Billy stays sleeping on the edge of the bed.

"I'll see you a minute, boy. Sweet dreams." With this, I turn the lights back off for him, before making my way downstairs and outside.

Mike is already waiting. The sun peeks up behind him, shining between the trees. We exchange a silent nod before we jog across Goodie Lane, diving into what's left of Bea's rosebushes. The last time we climbed through here, we were spying on Bea and Mrs. Smith, listening to their evil plot to kill me. The thorns sting just the same, even though the flowers have died.

"Scooch in closer," Mike whispers, motioning to the window. "It's open."

Together, we peer through the white panes into the living room. It looks the same as it did at the open house, with lots of neutral colors and mixed metals. An expensive-looking brown leather couch rests under the opposite wall, and I gasp as I notice Lex sleeping on it, wrapped up snugly in a blanket. Abigail and the other Ladies in White are nowhere to be seen.

"She spent the night on their couch?" Mike whispers the words with disgust.

I eye him. "Now do you believe me that they're weird?"

"Where are the rest of them? Did they go home?" he asks.

"Looking for us?"

I jump at the sound of the voice. I know who's standing behind us, and my body feels like it's been doused with ice water.

Mike's eyes widen, but he tries to stay calm. "Ladies," he says, spinning around with a fake smile spread across his face. "Good morning!"

Eleanor, Jade, Brea, and Cami stand behind us. They're all dressed fashionably despite the early hour—not a hair out of place, not a smudge in their makeup. They stare down at us with hard eyes and their hands on their hips.

How did they all get here so fast? I wonder. *They live in separate houses . . .*

"Care to explain why you're peeping through Abigail's window?" Jade asks. Her words have enough bite to make me take a step backward. The rosebushes absorb me, their thorns pricking my skin.

"We were just . . ." Mike pauses a beat too long. "We were just checking out the roses."

Jade arches a brow and exchanges a look with Eleanor. "The roses. Really."

"Really," Mike says, the lie rolling off his tongue. "Quinn and I started a little landscaping business around here. And roses are our specialty." He grins.

Jade snorts in response, but one corner of her mouth turns up as if she's amused by Mike's antics. "A *landscaping* business," she repeats, pointing between Mike and me. "The two of you?"

"Oh yeah! You name it, we'll do it." He begins listing jobs on his fingers. "Mowing, planting, watering, weeding, trimming. *Raking*." He nods toward the scattered leaves covering the yard. "Looks like she could use help with that at least, am I right?"

The Ladies in White don't answer. Mike bulges his eyes at me, begging me to corroborate his story. But I'm too taken with Cami to build on his lie: the closer I am to her, the more I notice that something is off about her skin. From far away, she looks fine—just a young woman wearing a tense smile. But up close, her skin changes—not the color, but the *form*. It flickers like candlelight, and for a second it's almost like I can see right through her. She takes a step closer, and I gasp as a shadow stretches out like wings behind her back.

"Quinn?" Mike asks, pulling my attention toward him. "She's just shy," he tries to explain. "You know, meeting new people makes her kind of freeze up sometimes. Give her a minute, and she'll be chatting us all to death." He laughs a little too loudly.

Brea cocks her head to one side. She moves forward so that her body covers us with its shadow, which seems impossibly long and large for such a thin woman. Her eyes darken until they resemble coals, and her skin starts to flicker just like Cami's did moments before. It feels as if I'm outside without a coat in the middle of winter. I can feel the ice in my lungs and the painful shivers down my spine. *"Parker?"*

I half-expect to see my own breath when I utter a word: "Huh?"

Mike flashes me a weird look before turning back to our neighbors. "So we're cool?" he asks. He fidgets beside me, and I can feel his nerves.

Brea steps back, her shadow shrinking and her eyes lightening. She sighs and spins around. "Let's go, you two."

"Go? Go where?"

"You wanted to see Abigail," she says. "So let's go see Abigail." She begins to make her way around the side of the house toward Abigail's front door. Jade and Eleanor follow behind her, and Cami gestures for Mike and me to go ahead, making sure we get in line.

Nothing about this feels optional, and my stomach tightens as we snake across the lawn, climbing the steps to Abigail's door. Brea doesn't bother to knock; she simply turns the handle and pushes through, leading us into the foyer with the black-and-white-checkered floor. At once, I feel another rush of cold, as though we suddenly landed in the dead of winter.

Mike is still chattering away, trying to convince Brea

that we don't need to meet with Abigail. "We can just drop off a flyer. We don't want to bother her."

His voice must carry through the house, because, all of a sudden, Abigail and Lex enter the foyer. A tiny yelp escapes my lips before I can swallow it. In all of the turmoil, I'd almost forgotten about Lex.

"Quinn? Mike?" She blinks her eyes as is she's trying to make sure that she's fully woken up. Her short hair is mussed up and sticking out in all directions, and she's wearing the same clothes that she wore to school yesterday. "What are you doing here?"

"We caught them in your rosebushes, Abigail," Brea says before Mike or I can answer. "They were looking through the window."

A hand flutters over Abigail's heart as if she's shocked. The gold locket catches the light from the chandelier above our heads, and for a second her skin seems to sparkle. "Surely you don't suggest that these darlings were *spying* on me?"

"Us? No," Mike interrupts, stepping in between Brea and Abigail.

"Then were you spying on *me*?" Lex asks, her eyes narrowing.

"No!" Mike says, but Lex waves him off.

"I'm talking to Quinn." She looks at me in a way that I don't recognize, in a mixture of hurt and betrayal.

I try to deny it, but it's like my mouth can't get the lie out. I'm left standing helpless in front of her, shaking my head.

"Now, Alexa, I'm sure there's a reasonable explanation for this," Abigail says calmly. "Quinn here is one of your oldest friends, is she not?" Lex shrugs. "So why would she spy on you? That's outlandish." She laughs. "I mean, no friend on earth would do such a horrid thing, would they, Quinn?" Her gray eyes lock onto mine, and I see a glint of amusement, as if she's enjoying the drama unfolding in her doorway.

"Lex . . ." I start, before trailing off again. I sigh. "Why don't you just come to my house? We can talk there."

"I think we're done talking," she answers, before turning on her heels and walking away from the doorway. I start to follow her, but Jade, Eleanor, and Brea block my path. Cami remains at Abigail's side, glaring at Lex in a way that makes me shiver.

"I think some space is in order," Abigail tells me. "Wouldn't you agree?"

Mike grabs me by the shoulders. "It's cool, Parker, we can just talk to her later." He pulls me toward the door, which Brea holds open for us. Together, we bolt across the street.

"We can't talk now," Mike tells me, shooting a look toward Abigail's house. "We'll have to wait until we walk to school." He checks his watch. "I'll see you outside in half an hour."

I nod, my hands still shaking as I turn around and race inside, locking the door behind me. Billy is waiting and barks when I come in, and I fall on the floor beside him, burying my face in his fur. *What just happened?* I still can't believe we got caught—Mike and I never get caught, not even last summer when we were sleuthing all over South Haven. It was almost like the Ladies in White were waiting for us, and Abigail was all too eager to call me out in front of Lex. It's like she *wanted* us to fight.

After one last pat on Billy's head, I pull myself to my feet. It's time to rally.

I dress with a strategy, choosing an entire outfit that Lex gifted me for my birthday over the summer. I even take the time to put some product in my hair after my shower, so that by the time it air-dries, it falls into neat waves along my shoulders. Looking in the mirror, I barely recognize the trendy, put-together girl staring back at me. If there's any semblance of my friend left in Lex's body, this outfit will demand her attention. And maybe—just maybe—the gesture will help me with my apology. I give my hair one last *zhush*, but before I turn away, I notice something over my shoulder. It's a shadow, only it's not *my* shadow.

"What the—"

I spin around to face my empty room. Billy nuzzles against my shins. "You saw it, too, didn't you?" I ask him. His old eyes seem to say *yes.*

I do a quick sweep, ending in front of my dresser. Dad's picture is perched on top of my jewelry box. *That's strange.*

I'd never balance the frame on top of the lid like that. Just as I reach out to move the picture back where it belongs, the overhead light starts to buzz and flicker. Billy howls. I drop the picture, and both of us run from the room. I hover for a second at the bottom of the stairs, staring up into the empty hallway, trying to catch a glimpse of a shadow, a light—*something.* But there's nothing.

The chill stays with me until I'm back outside with Mike.

"Whoa," he says from the sidewalk, his eyes shifting over my outfit and my hair. "Why so dressed up?"

"Lex bought me this shirt," I explain, slipping my backpack onto my shoulders. "I thought it might help me win her over today."

"I don't think I've ever seen you without a ponytail," he continues, tugging on the edge of my waves. "It looks"—he waits a beat before deciding on a word—"*nice.*"

Warmth stretches over my face and neck as I duck out of his reach. "So what's our next plan?" I ask, desperate to change the subject.

"You mean because our first plan failed so miserably?"

We begin to walk, throwing nervous glances over our shoulders as we pass by Abigail's house. I wonder if Lex is still seething inside, or if Mrs. Vega finally dragged her home.

What happened earlier wasn't my mind playing tricks on me because of hypervigilance. It was real. As real as

Mike's favorite blue hat. As real as the shadow I saw earlier in my room.

I shake it off, turning to Mike. "The plan wasn't a total failure. Our goal was to find information. We found information."

"*What* information? What did we find out that we didn't already know, Parker?"

"That Lex stayed the night. That Abigail is trying to drive a wedge between us."

Mike is shaking his head. "She isn't trying to drive a *wedge* between you guys. She was just calling us out for spying. I mean, she kind of had a point. *I've* never spied on any of *my* friends before . . ."

"Whatever. Lex is your friend, too," I tell him. "And you can't tell me that Abigail didn't look happy when Lex left the room. I'm telling you, Mike, she's trying to isolate Lex."

"Don't you mean *Alexa*?"

I whack him in the arm. "See? That was weird. Not even Lex's mom calls her that. And didn't you see their bodies flicker?"

He waves me off. "Trick of the light."

"I *know* something's wrong. Come on."

"You have a feeling. But a feeling isn't evidence, Parker. We need something real."

I nod. "That's why we need a Plan B."

"Well, don't look at me for ideas. I thought you were taking the lead on this one."

"You should already know what I'm going to say."

Mike's groans. "Not the library."

"What's wrong with the library? We solved half of the Oldies' case there. You said we could research today."

"I just don't see what the point is. Why can't we just google stuff on our computers?"

I think it over before shrugging. "I guess that can work. We don't need the archives or anything this time."

"My house, then," Mike says. "Mom just went grocery shopping, so we've got snacks."

I roll my eyes. "Honestly, all you think about is food."

"I'm a growing boy. Besides, I need my brain food when I study. Research shows that if you snack while you work, your memory is better."

I shoot him a skeptical look. "I'm sure the study meant something healthy, like blueberries or peanut butter. Not spicy Cheetos."

He shrugs. "Don't knock them until you try them."

"Thanks, but I'll pass." I nudge him in the arm. "So, are you really in?"

"Yeah, I guess. But I don't think it's going to help much. What are you expecting to find?"

"Proof that Abigail is actually a ghost who is trying to possess our friend."

"*Possess* our friend? Come on, Parker. What would anyone want with Lex?"

"I don't know. Maybe they need a living person to do something. Remember how the Oldies needed me?"

The memory of the would-be sacrifice makes us both shiver.

I step closer to him. "We just have to figure out what they want and how to stop them."

He makes a face. "That's all, huh? Simple."

"Simple."

We approach the school, our feet crunching over the leaves, sending up an earthy scent. I breathe it in, feeling a little better knowing that we have a plan, or at least the start of a plan.

"Here we are," Mike mumbles, pushing open the double doors. He pauses and turns to me. "Maybe you should start by just talking to Lex. You know, ask her how she feels or something?"

I nod, following him into the crowded hallway. "I'll try."

And I *do* try in homeroom.

"Hi, Lex," I say as she comes in. She doesn't answer, but at least she still sits next to me.

My stomach tightens. "You have every right to be mad at me," I continue. "But I'm really sorry for this morning. It was stupid. Mike and I were just . . ." I let my words trail off as I notice that she's not listening. She's writing something in her notebook.

"Lex?"

She doesn't look up.

I peer over her shoulder. "What are you working on?"

Quickly, she covers the page with her arm, hunching over the notebook so that I can't make out a word. "Nothing."

Time to try a new tactic. "I'm wearing the outfit you bought me. See?" I pull on the edge of the shirt for emphasis. She still doesn't look up or answer—it's like I'm talking to a ghost.

I drop the fabric and feel my body grow hot. This was such a stupid idea. Of course she doesn't care about my shirt, and now I'm stuck wearing these trendy clothes that look ridiculous on me. I wish I'd just worn my favorite T-shirt and a pair of jeans. But then again, Lex *does* care about clothes, and when I unwrapped her present, she went on and on for twenty minutes just about the forest-green color and how *in* it was this season, and how it would complement my olive skin tone, and how I should wear a rose-colored necklace to pop against the green. At the time it was summer, and so I'd promised to wear the outfit after school started up again, and she'd beamed. For whatever reason, this silly outfit had mattered to her. Only now it doesn't. Part of it might be because of what happened this morning, but the Lex I know would never give someone the silent treatment, no matter how mad she was. The Lex I grew up with would follow you around, demanding answers *and* an apology. The cold, quiet girl in front of me? I don't recognize her.

The bell rings, and Lex takes off without a glance in my direction. I dig around in my pencil case until I find a spare elastic, yanking all of my brown waves up and out of my face.

Zoe is waiting outside for me in the crowded hallway. "Hey, nice shirt! Did Lex see it yet?"

"I'm not sure," I admit.

We step into Spanish class, and my heart sinks even further: this will be the first time I'm seeing Jess since the incident on the field. She trots in just before the bell rings and slides into a seat in the back of the room, about as far away from me as she can get. I don't dare turn around, but I feel her rage behind me, and it makes me dread track practice after school. I feel so on edge for the next forty minutes that I swear I'm in danger of spontaneously combusting by lunch.

Lunch! I don't know how I'm going to get through it without the other girls figuring out what's up.

Zoe notices right away that something's off. She eyes Lex and me across the table, taking in our stiff postures and untouched food. "What's wrong?"

"Ask *her*," I mumble before I can stop myself.

Lex's eyes flicker toward me. An awkward laugh rings out from the back of Zoe's throat, and I feel her kicking me under the table, desperate to get some kind of reaction.

Kaylee changes the subject. "So, I was thinking that maybe we could go to Harvey's after the track meet on Saturday?"

"I'm not coming to the meet," Lex says.

"O-K?" Kaylee says with a face. "But you never miss a meet."

Lex just shrugs.

"Maybe tomorrow, then?" Kaylee asks.

"I'm working," Lex says, her voice once again indifferent. She rips apart bits of her sandwich but doesn't eat any of it.

The four of us spend the rest of lunch in silence, the kind of silence that makes you want to pull up a hood and hide. Normally the thought of track practice later would make me rally enough to smile, or to joke with Zoe or strategize with Kaylee. But not this time. This time I have nothing to look forward to.

Track practice is worse than I thought, but at least it goes by quickly. Coach must have a heart after all, because he lets us out early without any explanation. Thank goodness, as none of my teammates will talk to me—well, except for Kaylee and Mike.

Mike meets me on the top of the hill after we change, and together we trudge forward until the field looks like a speck in the distance. We make our way down Main Street. The air around us feels heavy, like the dark clouds are about to break.

Mike's eyes follow my gaze up toward the sky. "It looks like it might storm."

"Then we'll run. Unless you're afraid that you'll melt in the rain?" I grin at him, throwing one of his old jokes back into his face.

"Nah. We destroyed the only witch in town, remember? I can handle a little precipitation." He pulls his hat down. "Let's go."

The air is even denser by the pond. It hovers, billowing in swirls just above the surface. We quicken our pace, speed-walking until we come out on the other side, then our feet slow down until we reach Goodie Lane. I tug down the sleeves of my hoodie so that my hands are half-covered in the soft cotton. Thunder rumbles faintly in the distance, and we bolt the rest of the way to Mike's house, not stopping until we practically fall through the front door.

Mike looks at me. "I thought you didn't care about a little old thunder, Parker?"

"I don't."

He smirks. "OK, whatever you say. Come on."

The Warrens' house is warm and cozy, with books practically everywhere. I follow him through to the dining room, where we set down our bags. Mike hands me his laptop while he goes to the kitchen to gather some snacks. He returns just as I pull up Google, and he slaps the bag of chips in his hands so that it makes a loud *pop* when it opens.

"Be serious," I tell him.

"Oh, I'm serious," he says, falling into a chair. "Serious about my *snacks!*" He drops the chips onto the table and pulls out two cans of soda from his pockets, handing me one.

"Let's get to work," I say.

Mike pulls his chair in closer to me and the computer. "OK, Abigail. Let's see who you really are." He reaches across and types in **Abigail Drout**. The Design on Goodie home page pops up as the first hit.

"No, not Drout," I tell him, tugging back the keyboard. "We need to search for her full name—the one written on her grave."

I type **Abigail Drout McClain** into the search. I hold my breath as a bunch of hits come up. I click the first one, which opens up an old issue of the *South Haven Times*. My eyes catch the headline: **Local Couple Marries! Mrs. Abigail Drout and Mr. Christopher McClain Marry in Downtown South Haven**.

The black-and-white photograph shows Abigail wearing a long, white lace dress layered with satin, a birdcage veil clipped in her hair, and a smile on her lips. She stands on the front steps of the oldest church in South Haven next to a man in a simple black suit. She looks so happy and alive. The date reads 1951.

"Click the next one," Mike tells me, his face suddenly serious.

I close the marriage announcement and open the next

link. Both of us suck in our breaths as we read the heading: **Tragedy Strikes in South Haven**.

The photograph below the headline shows Abigail again, but this time she isn't wearing a wedding gown. She stands beside a tall and handsome man who balances two little girls—one in each arm. The four of them are all laughing, as if the photo was taken right after someone told them the funniest joke in the world.

I skim the rest of the story. "Oh my gosh—they died! The little girls. They *drowned*."

"In the pond?" Mike asks.

"No. In the Flynn River. Apparently, it flooded really badly back in 1956. I guess there was a storm. The girls, Ava and Emily, got swept up in it when they tried to find their dog." Flynn River is at the other end of town, farther from the sea and closer to the forests that line the east end of South Haven. I remember learning about the Flood of '56 from Mrs. Davis in social studies. Lots of lives were lost.

"Oh my God," Mike says, taking off his hat and placing it down on the table. "Both girls?"

I nod. A sadness hangs heavy in the air. I can't help but stare at the smiling faces of the little girls in the photograph, neither of whom looks older than five.

"Poor Abigail. I actually feel kind of bad for her now," I admit.

"Does it say what happened to her?" Mike asks. "You know, after the drowning?"

"Not in this article." I exit the page and open another one. We both gasp at the headline.

Local Mother Drowns on the Anniversary of Her Children's Deaths

I look at Mike. "I told you. She's a—"

"Don't say it."

"Ghost!"

He shakes his head.

"You can't deny it now," I tell him, gesturing at the screen. Abigail smiles back at us in the black-and-white photo—the picture used in her obituary. It is, without a doubt, 100 percent our neighbor.

Mike places his face in his hands and takes a series of deep breaths. I wait for him to finish, twisting my fingers around the edge of my shirt.

"Are you OK?" I ask him. "Do you want to quit?"

He jerks his head toward me. "Quit? What are you talking about, Parker? When have I ever left an open investigation?"

"I just thought—"

"I don't quit anything. You should know that by now." He picks his hat up and tugs it back in place on his head. "I bet you the key is in the husband. If we figure out this Christopher guy, then we figure out Abigail."

My fingers start tingling, anxious and excited to find

some more answers. But as soon as I reach for the keyboard, the screen freezes.

Mike frowns. "What?" He takes the computer from me and tries hitting a few keys. When that doesn't work, he powers it off and then on, but the screen is stuck, frozen on Abigail's haunting eyes.

"Weird."

Just then, the front door opens, and in walk Mr. and Mrs. Warren.

"Oh, hi, kids," Mrs. Warren says. "Doing homework?"

Mike slams the laptop shut. "Yup. Homework."

"Do you want to stay for dinner, Quinn?" Mr. Warren asks. "I'm grilling cheeseburgers. I figure we might as well use the grill before it gets too cold out."

The word *cheeseburger* makes my mouth water. Mom and I haven't touched the grill since Dad died. The realization turns my stomach, and I shake my head politely.

"Thank you, but I should be getting home." I stand up and gather my things. "I'll see you tomorrow, Mike."

He follows me to the door. "Want me to text you in the morning? Before the track meet?"

Ugh, I'd forgotten about the track meet! My muscles tighten as I try to put on a brave face. "Sure. Thanks."

He smiles. "Later, Parker."

"Bye, Mike."

With this, I make my way home just as thunder starts to roll.

CHAPTER 9

The thunder continues throughout the night, threatening a storm that doesn't come. Part of me wishes it *would* storm; then I'd have a legitimate excuse to miss the track meet. My stomach twists and turns as I roll around in my bed, trying but failing to get comfortable. By the time my alarm goes off, my eyes are burning with exhaustion.

My phone vibrates on my nightstand. It's from Mike: *Good luck today*, he writes.

I don't bother to text back. I'm sure Mike can guess how I feel.

Instead, I get dressed, tugging on my Rocky Hill uniform with a heavy heart. Luckily, Mom's working, so at least I don't have to explain my feelings to her. Mike's parents offer me a ride, and in the car I keep my cheek pressed against the window, too embarrassed to even look at Mike or talk to anyone. The drive is over too quickly, and then I'm faced with the moment I've been dreading: the walk down to the track field. Kaylee is waiting for me by the gate. She joins my side and squeezes my hand.

"It's just one meet," she whispers, but the encouragement falls flat, and I can't manage an answer.

She then looks up at the sky, pointing out the dark clouds that still threaten thunder. "Maybe you'll get lucky and it'll storm and the meet will get canceled."

"I doubt I'll get that lucky . . ."

"Nope. Not having it, Parker," Mike says, interrupting us with a shake of his head. "Wipe that frown off your face. You can't let your teammates see you like that."

"What do you want me to do, Mike?" I mutter. "I'm barely on the team today."

"You're still a captain, Parker. You've got to cheer on your team."

"Sorry. I don't have it in me to be a cheerleader."

I start to turn away to head to the bleachers, but Mike cuts me off, blocking my path.

"You don't have a choice. You want your teammates to still see you as a captain? Or not?"

"He's kind of right," Kaylee says. "I mean, look at Jess."

My eyes scan over to the bench, and I see Jess hunched over with her hoodie drawn, hiding her face. Her arms are folded across her chest, making her look grumpy and so un-captain-like. She's not even wearing her uniform. The image causes me to take a sharp inhale.

"OK, you're right," I tell them. "Let's do it."

With this, Mike cups his hands around his mouth and yells, "Let's go, Rocky Hill!" before breaking off into a run.

I exchange looks with Kaylee, and then we both join him, charging forward, yelling wildly and waving our arms in the air until we join our teammates on the field.

"Let's go! I want to see you stretch!" I tell them, taking my position in front.

Without a word to Coach, I lead the stunned girls in a series of stretches and warm-ups while Jess continues to sulk on the bench. For a moment, I almost forget that I'm not running today.

"Nice enthusiasm, Parker," Coach tells me, placing a firm hand on my shoulder. "But you're still benched."

"I know, Coach. But I'm also still a captain, aren't I?"

He nods. "That you are." He pats me on the back, approvingly, and I plant myself right next to him on the sidelines.

Mike gives me a thumbs-up from across the field as I shout my lungs out, cheering on my teammates, helping them stretch and cool down, amping them up, getting them water—anything they need. Jess doesn't move for the entire meet. A huge part of me wishes that

I could just slump down next to her, buried underneath my hood. It's hard to stay cheery. A year ago, this type of thing would have destroyed me. But I'm not the same girl I was a year ago. If the Oldies taught me anything, it's that I'm stronger than I give myself credit for. And besides, this was my fault. I have to own it. So I keep on cheering.

Coach pulls me aside afterward. "I can tell that hurt," he says, his usually stern eyes softening around the edges. "But I'm proud of the way you handled that, Parker. Next meet, you're running."

"Thanks, Coach." My face burns with both pride and embarrassment, and I don't admit how sick it felt to watch the other girls run in my events.

"And no more nonsense with you and Jess," he continues. "You're both co-captains, and I need you to start acting like a unit. No more of this competition garbage—save that for the field."

"Yes, Coach."

He walks away, and Mike takes Coach's place at my side. "You cool?"

I bite my lip. "Almost." I glance toward Jess.

He nods. "I'll wait for you by the hill. Good luck."

I take a deep breath and gather my courage before making my way toward Jess. The bench is cold as I take a seat beside her. She doesn't even acknowledge me at first.

"Hey." My fingers tingle like they do whenever I'm nervous; I twist them together. "Look, we deserved what we got today. Coach was right to bench us. We didn't act like co-captains."

I think I hear her sniffle under her hood, but I still can't see her face, and she still doesn't say anything.

"We need to do better," I continue. "We need to be on the same page and work together."

Still nothing.

"Jess?"

Thunder rumbles, and it makes us both jump. I realize that I'm running out of time before it storms. "Jess, I'm sorry," I tell her. "I was late, and you called me out on it, and I got mad. I was embarrassed and upset, but I shouldn't have said the things that I said."

Jess finally looks at me. "I'm sorry, too," she says, her voice so quiet that, for a second, I wonder whether I heard her correctly. "I shouldn't have bumped you with my shoulder. I—I just get in my own head sometimes ..." She trails off as rain starts falling.

"I get it." I nod. "We should probably go before it pours."

At this, we both stand up. Jess starts to head in the opposite direction, before spinning around to face me. "Are we cool?" she asks.

My muscles relax. "We're cool."

She doesn't smile, but neither do I. Still, a feeling of relief washes over me.

"I'll see you on Monday," she says. "You can lead the warm-ups."

"I won't be late."

With one last look at each other, she goes left and I go right, back over to Mike.

"You did good, Parker," he says as I approach. "I'm not saying you're Batman or anything, but that was definite Batman material."

I snort. "Thanks, Robin." I look around. "Where are your parents? Aren't they driving us home?"

He blinks. "I thought your mom was picking us up?"

"No. She's working."

"So are my parents. They left right after my first event. It's homecoming weekend, which I guess is a big deal." He shrugs at me. "It's just us, Parker."

Before I can answer, another clap of thunder opens the sky, and a sheet of rain starts to fall like a curtain.

"I guess we're running home," I say.

"You ready?"

"Ready."

We take off, our feet crashing through puddles as we charge ahead. The cold water coats my face, and it awakens me like nothing else. I've run in the rain before for track practices when Coach refused to cancel, but I've never felt as alive as I do right now. Together, Mike and I start racing each other, our hearts thumping in time to our footsteps. We keep running until we reach the pond, and we both jolt to a hard stop, our sneakers skidding in the soft mud.

"It's flooding," Mike says, noting how high the water has risen.

"Mom says the pond hasn't flooded since she was a kid."

"Doesn't mean it's not going to flood now."

A flash of lightning suddenly cuts across the sky, causing us to jump closer to each other. My eyes trace the strip of light to the old lightning tree, whose tired branches hang down over the pond.

"Is it true that lightning never strikes the same spot twice?" I ask.

"Nope, that's a total myth," Mike answers. "In fact, lightning is actually *more* likely to strike the same spot again. But don't worry—it was Sarah Goodie's magic that burnt the tree, not the sky. We're safe."

"We should still go," I say, not waiting for Mike to respond before I dart around the pond and toward the edge of the cul-de-sac. The curtain of trees bow beneath the weight of the water and the wind, reaching out their limbs as if to snatch something—or someone—below.

The rain pounds down harder around us as we make our way to my front steps. Mike throws a look over to his empty driveway. He hovers on my doorstep as I fumble for my key. "Hey, can I hang out here until my parents get home?"

"Yeah, don't worry, I'll protect you," I say, opening the door. He follows me inside and is greeted by a very nervous Billy. Billy hates thunder.

"Puppy!" Mike cries, dropping to the floor so that he can gently wrestle with Billy.

"He's too old for that," I scold Mike.

Mike pretends to place earmuffs on Billy's ears. "Don't listen to her, bud. You're not old."

His phone beeps. "It's my mom," Mike says, glancing at the screen. "She said they're going to hang out at the college until the storm clears."

I check my own phone to find three messages from my mother. "My mom's waiting it out at the hospital. She's trying to get hold of Grandma Jane so that she and Red can stop by."

Mike nods and looks from his own sopping clothes to mine. "Got a towel?"

"On it." I trot to the linen closet and grab a stack of clean towels, tossing two to Mike and keeping two for myself. For a few moments, we try to scrub ourselves dry, but my shirt and hair are still so soaked that I shiver. I look at him. "This isn't working, is it? How about I throw our clothes in the dryer?"

Mike's eyes widen. "Then what am I going to wear?"

"I'll find you a pair of sweatpants and a T-shirt." I raise an eyebrow. "Unless you'd rather stay wet and cold?"

"No," he grumbles.

"I'll be back in a minute. You can grab the chips from that cupboard, if you're hungry," I say, nodding to the corner cabinet before I make my way up the stairs.

I change quickly, savoring the warm clothes on my limbs. I towel dry my hair and let it fall down around my shoulders. Then I grab Mike a pair of baggy sweatpants and a Rocky Hill Track T-shirt and head back down. He nods approvingly at my choices and disappears to change.

"You're kidding," I cry when he emerges from the bathroom. "You can't wear a sopping wet hat, Mike!"

Mike shakes his head. "I can't let you dry my hat. It's my favorite. What if you ruin it?"

I roll my eyes and stick my hand out. "I'm not going to ruin it. You're going to get sick if you keep it on. Stop being a baby and give it to me."

Mike hesitates but eventually drops the Yankees hat into my hand. I bundle all of our wet clothes together and take them down to the basement so that I can drop them in the dryer. When I come back up, Mike is sitting at the table, stuffing potato chips into his mouth. I grab my laptop and notebook and join him.

"What's all this?" he asks.

"Ghost notes."

He throws his head back with an exaggerated sigh. "You want to research *now*, Parker?"

"Yes, *now*. We didn't finish the other day. And this is important! Have you seen Lex? She looks like a . . . Like a . . ." I trail off, unable to bring myself to attach the word *ghost* to my friend.

Mike pushes the chips away and pulls the computer toward him. "Fine, but do you have any cookies? I need some brain food."

"I'll look while you start googling."

"What should I start with?"

"I don't know. Maybe the husband? Christopher McClain."

"On it."

The sound of the computer keys tapping blends in with the sound of the rain outside. I find a box of chocolate chip cookies and bring them back to the table. Mike's already found something.

"Christopher was a traveling salesman, and he moved right after Abigail's death." Mike shrugs. "Can't blame him, though. I mean, he lost his entire family in this town. Why would he stay?"

"I don't know," I say, offering Mike a cookie. "But what about Abigail? Why in the world would she come back to South Haven?"

"She must be searching for something. Or someone."

I grab Mike's arm. "Does it say where the girls are buried? Emily and Ava?"

He scans back through the obituary. "Unity Cemetery."

"That's where Abigail's buried, but I didn't see the girls' graves when I was there." I can feel the pieces starting to fit together in my brain. "Spirits who return have unfinished business, right?"

"Allegedly."

"So maybe Abigail's unfinished business is finding her family?"

Mike nods. "And if she finds them, maybe she'll leave Lex alone?"

I can feel the hope thumping in my chest. "Maybe."

"But why wouldn't Abigail know where her girls are buried? They died before her."

"I don't know. But I think we should go to the cemetery and see for ourselves."

"Now?"

"No, not *now*. Tomorrow. Let's just see if we can figure out anything about the other Ladies in White."

Mike stuffs a cookie into his mouth. "You know their last names?"

I crunch on a chip and pull the computer toward me. "Here they are," I say, highlighting the four names on Design on Goodie's *About Us* page. "Eleanor Meehan, Jade Hendrickson, Brea Rao, and Cami Martinez." One by one, I drop the names into the search, frowning. A few hits come up, but none of them are the Ladies in White.

"Here, let me see," Mike says, reaching over and starting to type. "You've got to add the location. Didn't you say they moved around a lot? Where were the other design studios?"

"California, New Mexico, and Massachusetts."

"We don't know which woman is from which state, but we can try it a couple of different ways."

Our shoulders touch as I watch him type in all of the different combinations: **Eleanor Meehan + Abigail Drout** . . . **Eleanor Meehan + New Mexico** . . . **Eleanor Meehan + California** . . . **Eleanor Meehan + Massachusetts** . . . But nothing works.

"So either the Ladies have all changed their names or they're invisible online." He shakes his head. "None of it makes sense."

"Wait—click that one," I say, pointing to a link. "The one that says MISSING GIRLS."

Mike follows the directions, and both of us gasp as an article comes up. I clear my throat and read it out loud. *"Two local Long Beach teens go missing two days before graduation. Eleanor Meen and Jade Henders were set to begin school at FIDM in the fall. Both girls were last seen together on Belmont Avenue. Eleanor was wearing a blue cotton dress and gold sandals, and Jade was wearing green bell-bottoms and a yellow shirt. If you have any information, please contact Sergeant Zold . . ."* I trail off, quickly scrolling down until I land on the picture. I gasp. "It's them! They went missing in 1972."

Mike drops the rest of his cookie onto the table. "Type in their real names: Eleanor Meen and Jade Henders."

My fingers pound on the keys until articles flood the screen. My body freezes in the chair as I read the first headline: **Local Teen Girls Died by Poisoning**.

"Mike . . ."

"Let's try the next girl." He grabs the laptop and types in: ***Brea + missing + Massachusetts*** and ***Brea + missing + New Mexico***. Five articles come up. He clicks the first one: **Wheaton College Student Goes Missing in Norton, Massachusetts**. The picture is of a fresh-faced eighteen-year-old version of our third Lady in White.

"She went missing in 1998, and then her body turned up dead," he says, his eyes wide.

"How?" I ask, too afraid to read the words for myself.

"Poison."

Mike starts typing again as if his fingers are on fire: ***Cami + missing + New Mexico***. My knee bounces when he clicks the first link, and we come face-to-face with a school photo of our Cami. **Sixteen-year-old Taos Girl Missing Since Tuesday**.

"Was she poisoned?" I ask, holding my breath.

Mike nods and pushes the computer away. "A few years ago." Vertigo spins me around so that I fall against his shoulder; we remain like this for who knows how long.

"I think we need to tell someone," Mike finally whispers.

I sit up and face him, my cheek still warm from the heat of his shoulder. "No way."

Mike's eyes widen. "Parker, Abigail's a kidnapper and a murderer! This is bigger than we thought."

"But who can we tell? She's not just a kidnapper, Mike. She's a *ghost*. They're all ghosts! The police are never going to believe that."

He presses his thumbs against his temples. "So what do we do?"

A heaviness settles into my stomach as I flip open my notebook to the page on ghosts and place it between Mike and me. "I pulled this off a website. It talks about the different types of ghosts. Some can touch you and manipulate objects, while others are just an orb or a light. The Ladies in White must be poltergeists. Here, look." I type **poltergeist** into the search bar, and Mike makes a face as I pull up an article.

"This is ridiculous," he mutters.

I blink, using my sleeve as a tissue. "What is?"

"Look—this whole thing is just someone speculating. There's a list of ghost rules, but not any actual evidence. It's a joke. Listen: *Rule number one: there is no such thing* as a friendly ghost. All ghosts come from the same portal, so if you see a 'good ghost' or a lost loved one, be aware that demons may follow. Rule number two: be on alert. If you see a 'good ghost,' know that it might not be a good ghost at all, but a demon in disguise, tricking the living in order to gain entry through the portal."

"That can't be true," I say, skimming the article myself. "Some ghosts must be good."

"Not according to this." He sends the list to my printer, and I hear it churning out the document in the living room.

Suddenly a huge crash of thunder vibrates throughout the kitchen. The lights shut off, the computer shuts off, and we're surrounded by darkness.

"What the—"

I grab for my phone, turning on its flashlight. Mike does the same with his, and together we feel our way through the kitchen drawers and cabinets, fishing out real flashlights and Grandma Jane's homemade candles. Shadows flit around the room, causing me to jump every time I turn around.

"Calm down. It's just Billy. See?" he says, pointing to the black image on the wall, wagging just like Billy's tail.

"I knew that," I say, not meeting his eyes.

He just nods, before digging out an old pack of playing cards from the flashlight drawer. He waves the deck in front of my face. "You up for a game of War?"

"Seriously, Mike?"

"What? We can't just sit here in the dark, thinking about ghosts." He smirks. "Or are you too scared that I'll crush you?"

I snort. "As if you could ever beat me at anything," I say, leading him back to the kitchen table, armed with a second box of cookies and our lights.

Billy lies at my feet while Mike shuffles the cards, and I stare hard to make sure he's not cheating. He divides the deck into two even piles, and we immediately start flipping the cards onto the kitchen table—one by one—slamming them down so hard that my hand begins to hurt. Every so often, one of us notices a double, and we both yell out, "War!" We play game after game, neither one of us wanting to admit defeat, until finally I call a break so that we can get a drink.

"Don't open the fridge," Mike reminds me.

I freeze with my hand on the door handle. "Oh yeah," I mutter. We've been so into our card game that I almost forgot about the lost power and the storm. Instead, I move to the kitchen sink and pour out two glasses of water, handing one to Mike and downing the second one myself. Mike holds up his glass and inspects it.

"What, are you too good for tap water?" I ask.

"I was just thinking about the pond. I wonder if it's over-flowing."

I shrug. "I guess we'll find out tomorrow."

"You think we'll have practice on Monday if the fields are soaked?"

"Probably. Coach never cancels."

"It was pretty cool what you did today at the meet," Mike says, the compliment catching me off guard. "You know, apologizing to Jess? Dad is always telling me to be the bigger person, and that's what you were: the bigger person."

I soften at the praise, feeling myself blush. I'm thankful for the candles casting such dim light.

"I'm sure that was hard for you to be a cheerleader," Mike continues.

"Yeah, it was pretty much the worst track meet ever."

Mike steals a cookie out of my hand and stuffs the whole thing into his mouth. I whack him in the arm, our shadows dancing across the tiled floor. I grab my own cookie and settle back into my chair. Mike looks toward the window, watching the heavy rain continuing to fall.

"I wonder if the Ladies in White lost power, too. Or if the rain and the dark even bother them anymore."

My body stiffens at the mention of our neighbors. "Hear me out," I say, placing both of my hands on the table—something that Dad always used to do right before he said something important. "Something about this just doesn't make sense. Eleanor, Jade and Brea, and even Cami. They were all in their teens when they disappeared—they weren't little kids. And they live in houses of their own, have access to phones and computers. I mean, what's stopping them from contacting their parents back home? If they were abducted, why would they willingly stay with their abductor? Their *murderer*?" I watch Mike mull this over, but I keep going. "In fact, they all seem to worship Abigail—especially Cami."

Mike frowns. "Yeah, it's creepy. I don't like it."

"Me neither." Then a thought hits me, and my stomach drops. "Do you think Lex is over there right now?"

Mike's eyes widen, "I don't know. She's been over there every night, though, right? And Abigail hasn't done anything to her yet. I'm sure she'll be OK tonight, Parker."

That doesn't make me feel much better. "But she'll be next if we don't do something about it."

We allow the sound of rain to fill the space between us. It was different to hear the words out loud, and they make me shiver.

I'm the first to move, taking my flashlight to the living room to retrieve the printed ghost list. Then I return to the kitchen and set it on the table.

Mike eyes me. "We're back to this? Now?"

I nod and tap the paper. "Read."

Mike considers for a moment before pulling the candle closer to the page. He then holds the flashlight under his chin as if he's about to tell a campfire story; it illuminates his whole face, making his skin glow orange in the darkness as he reads. *"Rule number three: don't trust the movies. A sprinkle of holy water is not going to protect you from demons, nor will a cross, a Bible, or even a priest. In order to properly exorcise a ghost, you have to give the ghost what it wants. Sometimes, though, that's impossible. Sometimes, the ghost wants to cause pain."*

"Can you just read it normally?" I ask, interrupting Mike and swiping the flashlight. "Lose the Count Dracula voice."

"I was actually going for more of a Dr. Frankenstein voice."

"Frankenstein wasn't a doctor."

"Yeah, he was. Dr. Victor Frankenstein created a monster that most people call Frankenstein, but it's actually Frankenstein's monster."

I wave my hand at him. "Whatever, just keep going."

"Rule number four: arm yourself. If a ghost is in fact a demon, then it can hurt you (contrary to popular belief). How do I arm myself, you ask? Simple: with knowledge." Mike looks up and smiles. "I'm starting to kind of like this guy."

"Read."

"Listen for clues, follow in the ghost's footsteps, and talk to others who have come into contact with the same ghost so that you can compare encounters."

I hover on the edge of my seat as I process what he's saying, goosebumps lining my arms.

"Rule number five: get out. If the demon cannot be

persuaded to pass, you need to leave and get far away from it. If provoked, a demon can take hold of a human soul indefinitely. A demon can also kill."

This last line even gets Mike to show some emotion, having long lost the smug look on his face. We stare at each other above the candle as the room becomes inexplicably cold. The ghost rules fly off of the table as if taken by a gust of wind. I jump closer to Mike. Shadows crawl up the walls like giant black spiders, and this time, it's definitely not Billy's tail. They settle on the ceiling just above our heads, spreading out until they look like a murder of crows with outstretched wings.

"Mike..."

"Parker!"

Suddenly, there is a loud knocking on the front door. Billy jumps up and starts to howl, causing the shadows and the cold to disappear. Mike and I exchange looks before grabbing our flashlights and running to the living room. We peek through the blinds of the big picture window, desperately trying to see who is continuing to knock in the middle of this storm. My heart pounds like thunder.

"Quinn, honey, let us in!" cries a familiar voice.

My eyes widen. "Grandma Jane!" I quickly fling the front door open, ushering in a dripping Grandma Jane and Red, both sporting matching yellow ponchos.

"Your mother told me that you were alone, so we brought supplies. Be a dear and take these," she says, handing Mike and me a basketful of snacks, extra flashlights, and batteries. She pulls off her poncho, revealing a colorful sweater vest layered with crystal necklaces. She immediately takes a little bottle from her pocket and begins spritzing scented oil around the place.

"What are you doing?" I ask.

"Cleansing," she says, before recapping the bottle. "Now let's unpack."

After we move the supplies to the kitchen and hang their wet coats, Red hooks up a portable mini-generator so that we can charge our phones. "Never know how long the power will be out," he says.

Grandma Jane pinches his cheeks. "I love a man who's prepared."

Red blushes up to his hairline, his eyes twinkling in her presence.

Grandma Jane claps her hands. "Who's hungry?"

"I am!" Mike and I both say, despite the fact that we've already eaten our weight in chips and cookies.

Grandma Jane unpacks a Dutch oven full of brisket, somehow still warm from the oven. She then pulls out a bag of freshly baked rolls, and together we build ourselves heaping sandwiches, which we eat with one hand while playing War with the other. Grandma Jane's laughter rings up high above the thunder, drowning out the rain and softening the fear rising in my stomach.

CHAPTER 10

The power switches back on around nine o'clock, when the rain dissipates to just a mild drizzle. It sounds like a song against the roof.

Grandma Jane and Red leave to check on Red's house across the street. Mike's parents and my mom won't be home for another hour because some of the roads are flooded, but Mike says he's going to head next door anyway.

"Dad wants me to see if our basement has water in it," he explains. "I can come back, though, if you want. You know, to grab my clothes and wait the storm out."

"It's cool. You don't have to. I can bring your stuff tomorrow, and I'll be fine for a few more hours."

He presses his lips together, and I can't help but think that he looks disappointed. "Thanks for letting me hang out here. See you tomorrow, Parker."

"Bye, Mike."

And with this he makes his way out onto Goodie Lane.

I close the door behind him. The house feels all at once too empty and too quiet. At least Billy waits for me in the kitchen.

"What do you think, bud? You up for some of Grandma's tea?"

He seems to smile, and I take that as encouragement as I remove the pewter tin from the cabinet, which is full of hand-tied tea bags that I made with Grandma Jane. I flip on Mom's small kitchen radio and bop my head to the music while I fill the kettle with water. There's something soothing about moving around the kitchen, and for the first time I kind of get why Grandma Jane likes cooking so much. I know that boiling water isn't really *cooking*, but I still see the appeal of preparing something on your own. In a way it's sort of like running: there's a task at hand and steps to follow, and you can lose yourself in the goal.

Before I know it, the water is boiled and the tea bag is steeping in the hot water, filling the kitchen with its earthy, citrus scents. I lean against the kitchen sink, watching the light rain fall past the window.

And then the lights flicker: once, twice, three times. I hold my breath, hoping that we don't lose power again. Billy whimpers at my heels.

"It's OK, boy. Grandma Jane is right across the street," I say out loud, trying to reassure the both of us.

I stoop to pat his head, when all of a sudden, a shriek of static cuts through the radio: it's so loud that Billy howls and I have to cover my ears with my hands. A shadow seems to descend upon us as the room becomes unbearably cold. Then the lights flicker three more times until they shut off completely.

"Billy? Here, boy!"

I run my hand along the counter, trying to find a leftover flashlight. I can hear Billy crying, but I can't feel him at my feet anymore.

"Billy?"

The lights turn back on, and the static cuts to a screeching halt. Instead, a Beatles track blares through the radio: "Let It Be"—Dad's favorite song. My entire body freezes. I haven't heard this song since Dad was alive, and the familiar chords seem to slice through my chest, splitting my heart open all over again. For a moment, I stop breathing. My eyes are spilling over, tears running down my face.

Billy starts to howl again, his voice low and incredibly sad, like he's in pain. The noise is enough to break my trance, and I reach over to pound the *off* button on the radio. The motion is too quick, and I knock over my mug of tea. It spills everywhere, the water burning my hands.

"Shoot!"

Still crying, I dump the mug and spoon and half-drained tea bag into the sink, turning on the faucet to drown out the sound of my sobs. Billy quiets down beside me, and I hold on to the counter to catch my breath. It feels like I've just sprinted ten miles, my chest is so heavy. I catch my reflection in the window, and I can almost see my dad staring back at me through my own eyes. I know I look like him—people always used to say that I was his twin. But what I'd give to *really* see him in this glass, offering me a smile, telling me everything's going to be OK.

The radio switches back on, playing "Let It Be" again at full blast, the light flickering in time to the beat. Billy bolts from the room, but I stand firm against the counter. I know what this is.

"Show yourself!" I call.

The lights continue to flicker. The music continues to play.

"Show yourself!" I demand again. "Show your face."

And as if by way of answering, the music stops. The lights turn back on. A mist settles over the window, like the film that coats the mirror after you take a hot shower. My heart is racing, but I don't budge, not even when I feel a puff of cold air on the back of my neck.

"Who are you?" I ask, ignoring the tremble in my voice.

An image breaks through the mist—a reflection in the glass. Only this time, it isn't my own face staring back at me. It's Dad's. His brown eyes, his freckles, his crinkled forehead. His smile.

"Daddy?"

I feel the tears choking my throat. I stretch my fingers toward him, but just before my hand touches the glass, his mouth moves.

"Quinn..."

"Dad!"

I launch forward, reaching for him. When I touch the window, the mist swirls until it fades into nothing.

"Dad?" I press my palms against the glass. "No—stay with me. Stay, Dad!"

But all I see is my own reflection staring back at me, my mouth twisted and my eyes spilling with tears. I want to see him again—I need to see him again.

Without a second thought, I grab my keys and run out of the house, stomping through puddles all the way to the Warrens' front door. I stand in the rain and ring the bell until Mike answers.

"Parker? What's wrong?" He pulls me inside, holding me by the shoulders. "Calm down. Take a breath. What happened?"

I hadn't realized how badly I was shaking until I feel him holding me steady. "I, I . . ." It's impossible to get the words out.

"Come sit."

I push him away. I don't want to sit. My bones feel too jittery to be still.

Mike holds my gaze. "What. *Happened*?"

He'll believe me, I think staring into his eyes. *He'll have to believe* . . .

And suddenly, the words come. "I—I saw my dad!"

I don't know what I'm expecting in return. But not this—not the long, painful silence that follows. By the time Mike speaks, I'm almost surprised by the sound of his voice.

"What do you mean, you *saw* your dad?"

I wring my hands together, turning my knuckles white. "His face was in the window, in the kitchen. I was just having tea and—"

Mike shakes his head, cutting me off. "Quinn—"

"Why are you calling me *Quinn*?" I ask. My skin suddenly feels hot all over.

"Parker." He sighs. "Parker, look."

"You don't believe me!" I start backing away from him, dodging his outstretched hand.

"You didn't see your dad," he says, his voice full of sadness and regret, like he doesn't want to be saying his own words. "You probably saw your own reflection."

"No . . ."

"You said so yourself that you look alike, Parker."

"You don't know what you're talking about!"

"Look, it's been a long night. I'm sure you're tired and—"

"I'm not seeing things! It was him! Mike, I swear."

He stuffs his hands in his pockets, and the two of us face off against each other. I can hear the rain outside, each pitter-patter like a drum beating inside my chest.

Mike is the first one to break the stare. "Hold on," he says, disappearing into his kitchen for a few seconds, leaving me to drip in his doorway. He returns moments later, holding the article that he printed earlier at my house. "This guy—this ghost *expert*—says that there's no such thing as a friendly ghost."

"You said this article was ridiculous," I remind him.

"But it's not one article. I've been looking up more since I got home, and they all say the same thing."

I stiffen. "So?"

"So. If you really did see your dad—and that's a huge *if*— then it might have been a demon tricking you. It might have been Abigail!"

"That's not true. I'd know the difference." I picture Dad's face and the warmth from his smile. "It was him. He must want to tell me something."

Mike is shaking his head again. "No, Parker." His voice is low, just barely above a whisper. "It wasn't your dad. Everything I've ever heard says that spirits linger when they have unfinished business, or if they died in some sort of traumatic way. Your dad was loved. He had a good life. He wouldn't have any unfinished business here."

"*Me*—I'm his unfinished business!" I cry. "Doesn't he miss me? Doesn't he miss me enough to come back? Even just once?" I hate how broken my voice sounds. My legs turn into rubber, and it suddenly becomes difficult to stand up straight. "If ghosts are real, why can't he be real?"

Mike leans in closer to me, his warm eyes serious and melting into mine. "Parker." His tone is soft yet authoritative—the same kind of tone my mom used so often when she tried to get me to eat or clean my room right after Dad passed. "Your dad loved you. I'm sure that makes it feel like he's still here."

I bite my lip to keep from crying, but the tears begin to fall regardless. There's no hiding them this time. *But I feel more than a memory*, I want to say. My mind recounts the flickering lights, the found keys, the gusts of cold air, the shadow in my mirror. I look at Mike as he squeezes my hand. "I saw him," I insist.

"You saw something. But it wasn't your dad."

"Stop saying that!" I'm yelling, but I don't care. I drop his hand. "You never believe in anything. All you talk about is science and evidence, but you don't even believe the truth when it's staring you in the face."

"Parker, calm down—"

"Don't tell me to calm down!"

I'm shaking, but not for the same reasons as before.

Anger surges through me until I feel as if I might burst. I can't be in this house anymore. I turn for the door.

"Parker!"

I don't wait, I don't look back. I don't stop running until I'm at home, back in my kitchen, begging for my dad to show his face again.

I'm still standing in front of the window by the time Mom comes home. She finds me frozen at the sink, sobbing into a dish towel. Without a word, she takes me into her arms and guides me up to bed.

"It's OK," she coos. "I'm home now."

But nothing is OK. Nothing has been OK since Dad died, and I don't know when things will ever be OK again.

I can't stop crying, and Mom stays with me, whispering all the right words into my ear. "It's natural to miss him," she says. "Some days will be worse than others. Just when you think you have a handle on the grief, it sneaks up behind you and bites you again."

"I'm sick of feeling like this," I sob. "I just want him back."

Tears glisten in Mom's eyes as she kisses each of my cheeks. "I know, baby. I know."

She pulls the blanket up to my chin and strokes my hair until I cry myself to sleep.

CHAPTER 11

I wake up alone, my ears perked as they listen for the rain. All is quiet. All is still. My lungs ache from a night spent trying to catch my breath. My feet drag as I head down to the kitchen, where Billy is waiting without so much as a tail wag. I bend down to pet him.

"Hey, bud. Looks like you had a rough night, too."

When I stand up, my knees crack, and I stretch my arms up toward the ceiling. My eyes flicker toward the light, remembering the way it had flashed along to the beat of "Let It Be." The memories flood back. The shadows. The cold. Dad's face. My stomach tightens as I look to the window, expecting to see Dad's smile in the glass again. But nothing's there.

My phone buzzes in my pocket. It's Mike. I notice that he left a dozen messages last night, and two this morning. The latest one has an image of a sad otter, which makes me say "Aww!" out loud even though I'm still supposed to be mad.

I know you're there, Mike types. **I can see the dots! Can we just talk?**

I lean against the sink, gazing out into the yard. The morning light exposes the damage from yesterday's storm. Mom must have left the TV on in the next room before she left for work, because I can hear the newscasters talking about a mass flooding: waters from the local ponds and rivers have invaded people's basements, destroying carpets and hardwood floors. Most houses are still without power, but ours seems to be back. I squint toward Mike's house: his has power, too. It's almost as if Goodie Lane has its own little bubble around it. I can't help but wonder if I have old Bea to thank; she was a witch, after all, and Goodie Lane was her home for years. Is it possible that at some point she cast a protective spell over our street, like a giant umbrella?

My phone goes off again. **Parker! Just come outside. We still have a mission, remember?**

My stomach lurches. He's right! We're supposed to bike over to the cemetery before my mom comes home from her shift.

Give me five minutes, I type back. Then I head up to my room to change. Quickly, I dress in a pair of black jeans and a black sweatshirt, tugging on my lucky pair of running shoes. I leave my hair down and hide my face beneath the oversized hood. I then tuck Grandma Jane's crystal into my pocket and spritz myself with her homemade oils; she said they're for my protection, and I can use all the help I can get. I remember our conversation about magic, about the importance of trusting your instinct. *I sure hope she's right.*

Finally, I grab my backpack from the corner of my closet. It's already loaded up with supplies—granola bars, a fold-out map of South Haven, two bottles of water, and, of course, a bag of gummy bears. Billy watches me as I pull the straps over my shoulders. It feels like I'm forgetting something . . .

"His clothes!"

I race downstairs and take Mike's clothes out of the dryer. For a second, I hold his Yankees hat in my hand, and the betrayal that I felt last night slowly starts to dissipate. I hug it to my chest and put my game face on. Then I leave Mom a note, toss Billy a biscuit, and head out the door.

Mike is waiting for me in my driveway, wearing one of his ten thousand other Yankees hats. His eyes widen when he sees me, as if he didn't believe that I'd show up. We just stare at each other for a moment, letting the leaves flurry around us. Finally, I hold up his hat like a white flag.

"Truce?"

A smile breaks across his face. "Truce." I give him back his clothes, and he tucks them into his own backpack.

"Let me just grab my bike," I tell him, starting for the garage, but he stops me, pulling gently on my arm.

"Hey, Parker," he says, his voice, for once, uncertain. "I really am sorry."

He looks so sincere that it makes me blush. "It's fine," I tell him, even though I'm still not sure if it *is* fine. All I know is, he means his apology, and we have work to do. "I'll just be a second."

"I want to cut through the woods first," Mike says when I return. "Scope out the rest of the damage."

I nod, and together, we walk our bikes down the cul-de-sac. Goodie Lane might be safe from flooding, but the windblown leaves seem to coat every inch of the ground, making the grass look like a colorful quilt. Trees were split in half, their heavy branches littering the streets along with piles of dank red and golden leaves. At the end of the road, we weave through the trees until we reach the pond. Last night, the water had seeped over the brim, soaking the surrounding area. It's since gone down, but the embankment is still covered in a thick, stodgy mud. I shiver, wondering what might have washed ashore last night. Almost immediately, I think of Bea's mother, and I squint against the pond, half-expecting to catch a glimpse of the same orange light that lured me in over the summer. The water itself is covered with leaves and branches from the nearby trees, causing the surface to appear swampy and green—thankfully, not orange, not glowing, not outwardly dangerous.

"Looks like your lightning tree survived," Mike says, pointing to the scarred tree bending just over the edge.

Crows sit in its branches, and I wonder if they're the same ones that Mike and I saw at the playground back before things became so complicated.

"Let's keep going," I say, and together we hurry around the pond and over to the neighboring streets.

Mike rips open a Pop-Tart wrapper with his teeth and extends one to me. "Breakfast? I made my mom get the kind with the sprinkles—I know you love sprinkles."

I accept it, touched by the idea that Mike thought about me while grocery shopping. I take a bite. "Thanks."

"OK," he says through a mouthful of pastry, "here's the game plan. We finish eating, then we have a snack, then—"

"You're impossible," I tell him.

He cracks a smile. "Impossibly *awesome*."

"How did I end up with you as my partner?"

He tugs on his Yankees hat as he stuffs the last bit of Pop-Tart into his smug mouth. "You can thank Goodie Lane for that."

I sigh and dust the crumbs off my shirt. "We should start riding. It'll save us time."

Unity Cemetery is at the opposite end of town, far from the rocky shore that borders South Haven. Unity is out near the edges of the forest, past the cobblestone sidewalks and the Gothic library that towers over the town center and where the Phoenix Funeral Home used to be. Since the Oldies were vanquished, the ornate building now stands vacant, waiting for someone else to dare to unlock its doors.

We pass all of this as we ride, playing "dodge the branches" for a while, biking around the fallen tree limbs, rolling our tires across dead leaves. I peddle ahead of Mike, leading the way as we turn onto a side street. Then we relax our pace a bit and begin to cycle in circles around each other, weaving back and forth across the street. The houses are lined up in tight little rows, with Halloween decorations expertly arranged along their front lawns: plastic skulls and bones, cardboard tombstones, cotton webs with menacing black spiders climbing up them. Halloween isn't for another month, but South Haven pretty much starts decorating for the holiday as soon as school is back in session.

"Hey, Parker. Check this out," Mike calls, popping his front wheel off the ground. He grins at me, expecting me to be impressed.

I snort. "Please. I learned how to do that in first grade." In one sharp movement, I tug the handles hard and lift up my own front wheel, peddling fast enough to pass him again.

Mike looks so shocked that for a moment I'm afraid he might fall. I laugh.

"Close your mouth, Mike. You should know by now how awesome I am."

He flashes me a full smile before snapping his bike back down. "I do know," he says, before taking off in front of me.

"Hey!" I cry, charging after him.

We race until we're neck and neck, and only then do we pull back and slow our pace, keeping our eyes peeled for Somerset Road. There, we skid to a stop in front of the Unity Cemetery sign, its name etched in stone to resemble the tombstones beyond the black iron fence. I feel myself shiver inside my hoodie, goosebumps lining my arms. My stomach turns into a series of knots.

"You OK?" Mike asks, studying me from under his hat.

I take a deep breath and nod. *You're doing this for Lex,* I think, bracing myself. "Let's go," I tell him.

We hop off our bikes and walk them through the entrance. Once on the other side, we let them fall against the soggy grass. Our eyes scan the uneven rows of tombstones, some dating back four hundred years. The oldest graves are easy to spot with their dark, rough stone, whereas the modern ones are larger, shinier, and more evenly spaced.

My feet move on autopilot, guiding us to my father's grave. I stand with my toes pointed toward his stone and the drooping flowers at its base. Mike slides his hand in mine, intertwining our fingers and squeezing. *Did you visit me last night?* I want to ask. Instead, I let my head fall against Mike's shoulder, until a gust of wind swirls around my hair.

"Come on," I say, straightening. "We've got a mission." I drop Mike's hand and start walking down the row.

"Where are we going?" he asks, trotting to keep up.

"To see Abigail."

I lead him to the back corner of the cemetery, beneath the tall trees that cast a shadow over the spread-out plots. Just like last time, it feels cold near Abigail's grave, and I shiver.

"Whoa," Mike gasps, taking in the words on the stone.

"I'm not going to say I told you so."

He snorts. "You just did, Parker. Anyway, what are we looking for?"

"The daughters. Emily and Ava, remember? Maybe there's a clue on their graves. Come on."

We circle the plots surrounding Abigail's, reading all the names at least twice before looping back. I study Abigail's grave, noticing how isolated it seems to be. The space around it seems almost unkempt, kind of like there used to be plots there or that it'd been dug up at some point. *Could their graves have been moved?*

"Parker, face it. They're not here," Mike huffs, stuffing his hands into the pockets of his hoodie.

I frown at him. "That doesn't make any sense. You saw the obituaries. They have to be buried here. Let's take another look. Just to be sure."

Mike's shoulders sag a bit, but he agrees. We trudge back over the soggy grounds, reading stone after stone. Still nothing. Eventually, Mike gently tugs on my arm, asking to go home. I don't want to—leaving would be giving up, and I just have this nagging feeling in the pit of my stomach that we're missing something.

"Come on," Mike says, leading me back toward the gate where our bikes are waiting for us. "Let's just walk for a little bit and eat the gummy bears."

"Your mind is always on food," I mumble, but I take the gummies out of my bag. We walk and steer our bikes down Somerset Road, passing the candy back and forth as we amble along the sidewalk.

We're almost to the end of the old, wrought-iron fence when I notice a large white house standing tall across the street, overlooking the cemetery. It has one of those South Haven historical homes plaques, stating that the structure was built in the 1700s. The name on the mailbox reads HUDSON.

It's strange, for as big as the house is, I hadn't noticed it before. It's even got its own little pond along the side and a small forest. The trees are beautiful with their twisting branches and changing leaves, but something rests beneath them. *Three* somethings. Dark and withered, sticking up out of the ground. I catch my breath, letting my bike fall to the pavement with a thud.

"What's wrong?" Mike asks, his eyes wide.

I can't answer, so instead I point. Mike follows my gaze.

"Is that?"

"I don't know..."

We exchange looks, forming an unspoken agreement between us. I pick my bike back up, only to balance it against the fence. Mike does the same with his, and we make our way across the street toward the little pond, breathing in the earthy scent of fall as we run across the scattered ruby leaves.

"Over here!" I call.

Mike joins me at the edge of the forest, where we both stand breathless, gazing down at the three graves: two smaller ones for Ava and Emily McClain, and then a larger stone, carved with the name Christopher McClain Hudson.

"Oh my gosh," I gasp. I turn to Mike, my fingers tingling. "Hudson?"

"He must have changed his name. Maybe even remarried."

"But why would he move the graves? Why would he take them out of Unity?"

Mike shrugs. "Maybe he didn't want to be away from his girls?"

"But why not take Abigail with them?" I feel a ball of ice forming in my chest. "Do you think she knows?"

"Probably not. Maybe this is what she's been searching for?"

It makes sense. If Christopher changed his name and moved his girls' graves, then Abigail would be forever searching for them.

A crow circles above us, its shadow stretching out and casting light away from the graves.

"What do we *do*?" I ask Mike.

"I don't know." He fumbles with his phone as he pulls it out of his pocket, before clumsily taking a few pictures, his hands visibly shaking. "Evidence," he tells me.

The sound of tires moving on gravel pulls us out of the moment, and we freeze with the realization that someone's home.

"Run!"

We bolt back across the yard, past the trees and the pond. Through my peripheral vision, I can make out an old woman being helped out of a black sedan by a lady in scrubs: a home nurse, probably. I recognize them from the last time I came to the cemetery.

This time, though, the nurse looks less friendly. She glares at us. "What are you kids doing in this yard? Hey! I'm talking to you!"

We run faster toward our bikes and are about to hop on, when a voice calls us back.

"You're being followed," the old woman says.

I freeze, turning to look at her. She is a tall woman, with well-groomed silver hair that swoops to the side. Her body is thin and slightly hunched as she balances over her cane. But there's a strength in her eyes, a fierceness that draws me in.

"I can see the shadow. The darkness," she continues. "I can help you."

Mike is shaking his head at me, his eyes pleading with me to start peddling away. But there's something about the old woman's face that makes me trust her. I drop my bike back against the fence and head toward the driveway.

"Parker, wait!" Mike calls. When I don't stop, he sighs and follows me.

The nurse squints at the old woman. "You sure about this, Gwen?"

The old woman nods. "Come along, children." Then, with one last look over her shoulder, she allows her nurse to help her inside.

"What are we *doing*?" Mike whispers, pressing his shoulder against mine.

"I don't know," I admit, before stepping through the entranceway.

The house smells like cinnamon, and for some reason that's enough to set me at ease. Grandma Jane once said that you can tell a lot about a person by the way their house smells. Still, I'm not oblivious to the whole *stranger danger* thing. By all accounts, following an old lady into her house could be the worst idea in the world.

But right now, my gut tells me that Mike and I are safe— that this is exactly where we need to be.

We're slowly guided through a museum of antiques and rooms covered in floral wallpaper, until we reach the back corner of the house.

"Steph, dear, would you mind making us some tea?" the old woman asks her nurse.

Nurse Steph looks skeptical about leaving us alone, but after getting the old woman settled into an armchair, she disappears to the kitchen.

"Please, children. Sit down," the old woman says, nodding to the sofa. "What are your names?"

"I'm Quinn," I say. "And this is Mike."

Mike plops down beside me, sinking me into the cushion. Our legs touch, we're so close together, but I make no attempt to move away.

"I'm Gwen Hudson. Christopher McClain's wife, may he rest in peace."

For the first time, I really look around the room, and I see framed photographs on every surface. The pictures seem to span many generations, but the one that catches my eye is an oversized print capturing what seems to be Mrs. Hudson's wedding day. The groom in the picture is undoubtedly the same Christopher who was once married to Abigail.

"Why did you call us in here?" Mike asks. His question comes out a bit rude, and I nudge him in the ribs with my elbow.

"You said we were being followed," I say, cutting in. "Did you see someone?"

Her eyelashes flutter toward the ceiling. "Not someone. Some*thing*."

"Parker, I really think we should go." Mike whispers to me.

I ignore him. "What kind of something?" I ask, my arms prickling with goosebumps.

Mrs. Hudson blinks before widening her eyes to the point where they look ghostly white. "The shadow girl."

Mike starts to stand up. "OK. We're done here."

I tug him back down. "What shadow girl? Please, tell us what you know. I think our friend is in danger."

Mrs. Hudson nods slowly as she digs her nails into the arms of the chair. "Yes. She most likely is. Grave danger."

Her eyes flicker over to the mantle. Beside the wedding photograph is a framed portrait of Ava and Emily that I hadn't noticed before. Both girls are smiling, their skinny arms thrown around each other. Hanging from their necks are two gold lockets, just like the one Abigail always wears. A sadness presses against my chest as I consider the weight of losing these girls.

"That's them, poor little Emily and Ava," Mrs. Hudson says, noticing my gaze. "I still have a box of their things in Christopher's study. He never liked to feel apart from them."

"Then why did he move away?" I ask, turning back to Mrs. Hudson.

"Because she wouldn't let him *go.*" She whispers the last word so that it twists into something sinister.

I gulp. "Are you talking about Abigail?"

Mrs. Hudson nods. "She'll never stop chasing him. Or them. She'll continue collecting shadow girls, trying to fill her dark heart."

"What do you mean?" Mike asks, his voice trembling with the question.

"Haven't you figured it out?" she asks. "She's taking those girls to replace the loves that she lost. To replace Ava and Emily."

"Because she can't find them," Mike whispers, nudging me in the arm. I nudge him back.

Mrs. Hudson nods and motions to the window, which overlooks the yard. "Christopher had the girls moved when we returned to South Haven."

"When did you come back here?" I ask.

She seems to think for a moment, trying to recall the exact date. "Somewhere in the late sixties, early seventies," she finally says. "Christopher and I had our own children together, and he wanted to be near Ava and Emily again."

"So you knew about Abigail?" I ask. "When you got married?"

"Of course." Then her eyes darken. "And I know that she's come home."

Her words seem to cause a draft in the room, as if a window has just been opened. I shiver.

"Do you . . . Do you know that . . ." I can't force myself to say the rest of the words.

"Do I know that she's a ghost? Yes, dear. Yes, I do." She bends forward, bringing her wrinkled face closer to us. "Listen to me," she hisses. "You need to stay away from Abigail. *Away.* Don't wave, don't say hello. If she comes toward you, you use those legs and run."

Her intensity unnerves me. "Are you afraid of Abigail?"

Mrs. Hudson sits back. "Of course, child. Everyone with a pulse should be *deadly* afraid of Abigail."

Mike and I exchange looks and press our shoulders even closer together. I hear the high whistle of the teakettle, and I know we don't have much time before the nurse returns.

A cat suddenly purrs from behind us, causing Mike and me to jump. It trots past the couch and leaps onto Mrs. Hudson's lap. She smiles and pets its silky black fur.

"Oh, Florence. You silly cat." The cat licks her hand in response.

"How did you find out?" I ask, desperate to keep the conversation on track.

"Christopher told me," she says. "He used to see her figure standing over the girl's graves in the cemetery. He was afraid that if he left the girls there, they'd never be free to rest in peace. So he moved them. And eventually, Abigail moved on. Or at least I *thought* she did."

"No," Mike grumbles. "She was just out stealing new daughters from other towns."

"And she's about to take my friend," I add. "And maybe my uncle."

Mrs. Hudson shakes her head, her eyes wilted with sadness. "I feel for you, dears. But I also feel for Abigail."

"She's a monster," Mike says.

"She's a mother who lost her children," Mrs. Hudson says. "I always wondered if it was wrong of Christopher to move the graves. I can't imagine what it must have been like for Abigail to go back to Unity and not find her girls where she left them. She doesn't know that they're here."

"But if we found their graves so easily, why couldn't she?"

"Why would she ever think to look here?" Mrs. Hudson asks. "She didn't know about Christopher becoming a Hudson—she lost track of him when he started moving around the country and changed his name to mine."

"We have to stop her," I say, my voice barely above a whisper. "I mean, it's horrible what happened to her, but we can't let her keep doing this."

For a long moment, we sit in silence, listening to Florence's purrs as Mrs. Hudson continues to pet her with shaking hands. Teacups clink in the next room. Mrs. Hudson's breaths sound rough around the edges, almost like she is struggling to breathe. When I think about what we have to do, I can't help but worry that we're bringing trouble to this old woman—trouble that she might not be able to handle.

"What can we do?" I ask, feeling desperate with the question. "How can we stop her?"

At this, Mrs. Hudson throws back her head and lets out a cackle that cuts straight through to my bones. "You can't stop a *ghost*, dear!" she says, her eyes wild as she speaks.

"But there's got to be a way," I plead.

"Not with this one. She's too strong. She's too powerful."

"We can't run," I tell her. "Our friend is in danger."

"Better her than you," Mrs. Hudson mutters.

I feel myself recoil at her coldness, but for some reason, it gives me courage. "I don't run from things that are scary." My voice sounds strong despite the butterflies in my stomach. I feel Mike's hand grip mine, and I squeeze back. "I'm going to save my friend."

Mrs. Hudson's eyes soften, glistening in the corners as if she's holding back tears. "Stay away from the shadows."

"Tea, anyone?" Nurse Steph asks, smiling with a tray of porcelain cups and a plate of cookies. Her smile fades as soon as she looks at Mrs. Hudson, whose breathing is heavy once again.

"Gwen, dear, what's wrong?"

"They'll never stop her . . . she's too strong . . ."

Nurse Steph sets down the tray and wraps a blanket around Mrs. Hudson. Then she turns to us. "I think you kids better go now," she says gently.

My legs feel like Jell-O, but I force myself to stand and follow her to the door. I can still hear Mrs. Hudson mumbling behind us.

"I'm sorry, kids," Nurse Steph says in the entranceway. "She's a haunted woman. Never did get over the loss of her husband. And now her mind is starting to go. Dementia," she tells us with a sad expression. "Don't take anything she says to heart."

"Thank you," I say.

"Yeah, thanks," Mike says, tugging me down the porch steps and onto the driveway.

When I look back, Nurse Steph has already closed the door, but I can see a shadow rising from the window.

"We've got to go," I tell Mike, before jumping on my bike.

Together, we ride. But no matter how fast I peddle, I can't seem to escape the cold that follows us home.

CHAPTER 12

When we break through the trees onto Goodie Lane, it takes a moment for my heart rate to slow down. I keep an eye on the white houses to my left as I hop off my bike, looking for a trace of the Ladies in White or their ghost mother, Abigail. All looks totally normal, but that doesn't make me feel any better.

Suddenly, a car horn blares behind me, causing Mike and me to jump and spin around. It's Grandma Jane and Red, waving wildly from the open windows of Grandma Jane's car.

"Yoo-hoo, darlings!" she calls. "Come help us carry the food into the house. I'll reward you with homemade honey buns."

Mike's eyes widen in delight. "You didn't tell me your grandma was cooking."

"I didn't know," I admit. I quickly brush past him, dropping my bike on the grass before helping Grandma Jane out of the car.

Mike opens the trunk and lifts out a large chafing dish. He grins. "This smells so good!"

Grandma Jane beams at him. "Oh, thank you, Michael. Will you be joining us?" She reaches out to readjust his hat. "It looks like you worked up quite a sweat. What were you two up to today?"

"We were just biking around town," I say, as I carry the slow cooker into the house.

Red holds the door for me. "Do anything fun in town? Harvey's?"

I try to keep my face straight. "No, just biking around," I say, before kicking off my shoes at the door and dropping off the Crock-Pot in the kitchen.

"Well, there's my girl," Mom says, making her way down the stairs with Billy at her side. She pulls me in for a warm hug, her hair still damp from her post-work shower.

"Hi, dear," Grandma Jane calls, hurrying over to kiss Mom on the cheek. "We brought the works. Come on, troops," she says to Red and Mike. "Bring those in here." She leads the way into the kitchen, where she begins unpacking and organizing the food. "Quinn and Mike, why don't you set the dining room table? Seven places."

I look at her. "Seven? Who else is coming?"

"Uncle Jack and his new girlfriend."

My body goes cold at her words, and I quickly exchange looks with Mike. "You mean Abigail?" I ask. "From across the street?"

"Seems so," Grandma Jane says, sprinkling coarse salt onto the honey buns. "Red ran into them at the coffee shop this morning."

"Jack seemed pretty smitten with her," Red confirms, stealing a glazed carrot from out of the chafing dish.

Mom pours herself and Grandma a glass of sparkling water each. "I personally couldn't be more excited about this," she says. "You think Jack will wear the red flannel shirt or the blue?"

"The blue, dear," Grandma says, gently swatting Red's hand away from the food. "You know he thinks it's his lucky color."

Mom snorts. "In that case, I'm hoping he wears blue pants, blue shoes . . ."

Red waves a finger. "You two better behave yourselves. Don't embarrass the poor man in front of his girl."

Grandma Jane widens her eyes innocently. "What do you take us for, honey? We'll be nothing but our normal, polite selves." She winks at my mom across the kitchen. My mom laughs.

Grandma Jane turns to me. "You OK, dear? You look

LORIEN LAWRENCE

like you've seen a ghost." She rubs my back, and the warmth from her hand brings me back to life.

"I'm fine," I tell her. "Come on, Mike. Let's set the table."

Silently, we each gather an armful of dishes and silverware, carrying them over to the dining room. My hands shake, making the dishes rattle together. Carefully, I place them down one by one. Mike and I work in silence before meeting at the head of the table. My fingers grip the back of my dad's old chair.

"What do we do?" I ask.

"We stay alert," Mike answers, his face all business, his usual smirk lost in the seriousness of the situation. "We watch her. We try to ask her questions about her past and see where we get. And smile as much as possible—we can't give ourselves away."

I nod as he speaks, my lips already trying to practice my most convincing fake grin.

"Not that big, Parker, or else you'll look like a weirdo."

I punch him softly in the arm, and then the doorbell rings.

"I can smell the food from out here!" Uncle Jack's voice bellows. "We're coming in!" Then, without waiting for an answer, the front door swings open, revealing Uncle Jack wearing his blue flannel shirt, with a white-clad Abigail standing beside him. He holds out his arms at me. "Quinnie!"

Normally, I would charge toward him for one of his famous bear hugs, but seeing Abigail in my house causes

200

my limbs to freeze. Mrs. Hudson's words flash back to me: *She'll continue collecting shadow girls, trying to fill her dark heart.* I don't remember the dining room feeling this cold a few minutes ago, but now all I want to do is run upstairs to grab an extra hoodie.

"Hey, Uncle Jack," I finally say.

He lumbers over, squeezing me so tightly that I almost can't breathe. "How's my favorite niece?"

"I'm good," I tell him, unable to keep my eyes off Abigail beside him.

Uncle Jack notices my gaze. "Hey, Quinnie, look who I brought!"

Abigail smiles, leaning in close to Mike and me. I can smell her perfume, a mix of musk and rosewater. "How are you both doing? Is school going well?" Her eyes narrow. "Any more *spying*?"

I don't answer, my throat clogged with everything that I know about this woman that I'm not supposed to. Mike clears his throat beside me.

"We're good. Just busy, you know? With track and everything."

Thankfully, Grandma Jane saves the day. She saunters into the dining room with her arms extended out to Abigail. "It's so nice to meet you. My, she *is* beautiful, isn't she, Jack? I'm Jane. And you look hungry! Come, come, let's get some hot food into you."

Grandma Jane whisks Abigail into the kitchen, where she introduces her to Red and my mom. The three of them come back with full plates of deliciousness. Grandma Jane waves to us. "Go ahead, sweeties. The food's on the counter."

"Don't have to tell me twice," Uncle Jack says, making a beeline toward the kitchen.

Together, we layer on piles of roast beef and glazed carrots, Grandma's famous green beans, and, of course, the salted honey buns.

"Can you invite me over every time your grandma cooks?" Mike asks, his mouth hanging open as we take our seats back in the dining room.

"Dig in, dig in," Grandma Jane says.

There are a few blissful minutes when the only noises in the room are the sounds of silverware scraping against plates, followed by murmurs of appreciation for Grandma's food.

"So when's the next meet?" Uncle Jack asks. "I'm sorry I missed the last one."

"No, you're not," I mumble, finally finding my voice. "I mean, it wasn't good."

"Why not, kiddo? Did you make the other team cry when they ate your dust?"

My ears prickle as I bow my head. "I was benched."

"What on earth were you benched for?" Uncle Jack asks.

"Just"—I sigh, trying to find the right way to explain

it—"not being a good captain. Jess and I got into an argument on the field."

"To be fair, Jess started it," Mike says. "It wasn't Quinn's fault."

"That may be so, but Quinn, you can't let people get the best of you like that," Mom tells me.

Uncle Jack waves his hand. "Nonsense, Frances. The kid's got to stand up for herself. You don't want the other girl to walk all over her."

Grandma Jane leans over and strokes the loose hair away from my face. "You have a feisty spirit," she tells me. "Just like your father."

Uncle Jack snorts. "Yeah, James used to get in a few scuffles himself back in high school."

"Like father like daughter," Mom says, her voice softening. She picks her fork back up and points it at me. "Just don't let it happen again."

"Don't worry. It won't." And I mean it.

"Perhaps we can both cheer you on next time?" Abigail suggests, smiling between Uncle Jack and me.

Mike chokes on his water. I force myself to nod. "That would be . . . *nice.*"

"Why don't you tell us about yourself, Abigail," Grandma Jane suggests, eyeing our guest from across the table. "What brought you to our little town of South Haven?"

"True love, obviously," Uncle Jack replies through a mouthful of meat.

Abigail smiles at him. "Something like that," she says softly.

At this, I kick Mike beneath the table. He kicks me back, before leaving the toe of his sneaker touching mine. I don't move my foot; if I'm being honest, I'm comforted knowing he's so close.

"Seriously, though," Grandma urges. "What made you decide to set up a business on Goodie Lane, of all places?" She laughs a little at her own question, but there's a seriousness in her expression—a seriousness that demands a real answer.

Abigail pushes a green bean around on her plate. I notice that she has yet to take a bite. "I used to have family here," she says. "I thought it might be nice to pay homage to that and come full circle."

"Oh, is that right?" Red asks. "What was your family's name? I've lived here forever. I might know them."

"It was a long time ago," Abigail admits, her voice far away.

"Try me—I'm old," Red says with a chuckle.

Abigail spears a carrot and cuts it into microscopic pieces; she then pushes them around on her plate as she talks. "I've just always liked South Haven," she says, avoiding Red's question. "It's close to the city, but it's quiet. It's near the sea, near the forest." She smiles at Jack. "It's a great town to raise a family."

I half-expect Uncle Jack to balk at this not-so-subtle hint, but he just smiles at her as if they already have their whole future planned out. I shoot Mike a look, and he bites his lip in response.

"Where were you before this?" Grandma Jane asks. "I think Jack mentioned that you're coming from California?"

Abigail shakes her head. "New Mexico. Have you ever been there? It's beautiful."

"I'm sure it is," Grandma Jane says. "Why'd you leave if it was so beautiful?"

"Jeez, Janie," Uncle Jack cuts in. "Can you relax the interrogation for a bit? Let Abigail enjoy your delicious cooking?" He shovels a large hunk of bread into his mouth.

Grandma Jane holds up her hand. "I'm sorry—you're right—I'm sorry." She smiles at Abigail before turning back to Jack. "Chew, dear. We don't need you choking again like last Christmas."

"That was barely a choking!"

Mom eyes him. "I had to give you the Heimlich maneuver!"

"Just a little bit of the Heimlich. Come on, guys." He shakes his head and takes another big bite. "*So* good, Janie."

"I'll pack you up some leftovers so that you can have a sandwich for lunch tomorrow." She looks at Abigail's plate. "Are you not hungry, dear? You've barely touched it."

"It's absolutely delicious," Abigail insists. "I just had a big lunch." She smiles, and Grandma Jane smiles back, but neither one looks genuine.

I feel Mike's foot tap against the side of mine. I tap back, and for a second it feels as if we just invented our own version of Morse code: one tap for ARE YOU HEARING THIS? Two taps for SHE'S LYING. Three taps for I'M SCARED.

An awkward silence hovers over the table before Red clears his throat. "How about that weather, huh? Some rain. I won't have to water my tomato plants for a while."

"Did you see that the pond flooded?" Mom asks.

Red nods. "The Flynn River, too."

"The Flynn River?" Abigail asks. Her voice breaks with the question, and for a moment she looks so incredibly sad that I find myself feeling sorry for her. Mike and I exchange looks as she tightens her fingers around her locket.

"It's not so bad," Red tells her. "Not like when it happened in the fifties."

I didn't think it was possible for Abigail to turn any whiter, but for a moment she appears translucent and the room becomes even colder than it felt when she first arrived. I look to Grandma Jane to see if she noticed, but she's already up, clearing the plates.

"Victoria sponge cake, anyone?" she asks.

"Oh, Janie," Uncle Jack cries. "You just said the magic words."

"Quinn? Will you help me in the kitchen?"

I jump up, gathering the dirty dishes and following her into the next room. Once by the sink, Grandma turns the water on so hot that steam fogs up the window. I can't help but think of Dad's face staring back at me the other night.

"Grandma Jane?"

"Yes, dear?" She continues to move around the kitchen, pulling out a tall sponge cake and a bowl of homemade whipped cream. "Can you grab those strawberries?"

"Sure." I go to the fridge and take out the containers of fruit, setting them down on the counter.

"Slice them in half," she instructs, handing me a knife. "Then we'll decorate the top."

I start slicing, working up the courage to ask her my question. She studies me over the top of the cake as she starts piping on the cream. "Something wrong, honey? What did you want to talk about?"

My heart thuds. "Nothing really," I lie. "It's just— do you . . ."

"Spit it out, Quinnie."

"Well, you know how we were talking about your powers?"

"My *instincts*, but yes, go on."

I keep my gaze focused on the strawberries. "Do you believe in ghosts?" I blurt, the question tumbling out of me before I can word it differently. "Like, have you ever been able to, you know, talk to the dead?"

Grandma Jane seems to freeze, her hand mid-pipe. Her face softens behind her glasses. "Oh, baby girl," she says, her voice full of emotion. "Is this about your dad?"

I don't answer. I let her drop her piping bag and wrap her arms around my shoulders. "He's with you, you know," she assures me. "I feel his presence every time I look at you."

"But can you *talk* to him? Or Grandpa? Or anyone?"

"I talk to them all the time," she says. "But not the way you're thinking. It's more like a *feeling*."

I pull back and look at her. "So you've never seen them?"

"Goodness, no, Quinnie. I told you—I'm not that kind of witch." She frowns. "Why are you asking all of this? Did something happen?"

I want to say yes. I want to unleash all my secrets and ask more questions—like a hundred more questions. But in this moment, Red enters the kitchen, pulling Grandma Jane into a clumsy waltz across the tiled floor. Grandma tilts her head back and laughs, and for a second they both appear so young.

"That's enough, you old fool," Grandma Jane tells him, swatting him playfully with a dish towel. She turns back to me. "Now, dear, what were you saying before we were so *rudely* interrupted?" She winks at Red.

I swallow my words. "Nothing," I say, forcing a smile. "I'm good. Besides"—I nod to the cake—"we've got dessert to serve."

"Yes, I worry Jack will eat the tablecloth if we make him wait any longer," Red jokes.

Grandma Jane picks up her piping bag and continues to squeeze cream onto the cake in little dollops that look like clouds. I hand her a tub of rainbow sprinkles, and she smiles as she scatters them on top.

"Wow, Jack sure does seem smitten with Abigail, doesn't he?" Red says, stealing a strawberry from my pile and popping it into his mouth.

"What do you guys think of her?" I ask, lowering my voice so that I won't be heard in the next room.

"She has no taste in food, I can tell you that much," Grandma Jane mutters, eyeing her cake. "But she seems nice enough."

"Not as nice as you," Red tells her with a smile. He turns to me. "Did your grandma tell you that I'm taking her on a cruise?"

I blink. "What?"

"Yup. Right after the holidays. We're going to be cruising around the Caribbean, dancing under the stars." He spins her around again, and she looks so incredibly happy in his arms. And carefree. I realize that I can't tell her about Abigail and the Ladies in White. I can't ruin her happiness, and I can't risk putting her and Red in danger again like I did with the Oldies.

"Jack sent me to check on the cake situation," Mike says, popping his head into the kitchen.

"I've got it," I say, picking up the platter. "Can you grab the strawberries, Mike?"

We return to the dining room with the cake. Everyone takes a slice—even Abigail, though she only pushes it around her plate, like with dinner, and never once brings her fork up to her red-touched lips. But we end up devouring more than half of the cake, before leaning back in our chairs.

"Well," Uncle Jack says, pushing himself out of his chair with a grunt. "That was one of the most delicious dinners in the history of dinner, Janie."

"I'm so glad you enjoyed it, honey," Grandma Jane says.

Abigail stands up, too. She smooths out her skirt and takes a step closer to Uncle Jack. "Thank you so much for having me. I had a wonderful evening."

"Any time, dear."

My mom nods. "Yes, please, don't be a stranger. And take care of this lug." She whacks Jack in the arm.

Abigail nods. "I intend to."

She turns, setting her cold eyes on me. "It was so nice to see you, Quinn. Alexa talks so much about you that it feels as if I've known you forever." Then, before I can move out of the way, she pulls me in for an unwelcome goodbye hug, her body as stiff as a rock and just as cold. The hug seems like a threat—like a warning. I can feel her unspoken words as she squeezes me tightly: *Leave Alexa alone!*

I gasp for air just as Uncle Jack breaks us up. "Okay, okay, my turn. Let me get in on this bear hug." With this, he peels Abigail off me and wraps his own arms around my shoulders, bringing warmth and life back to my bones.

Mike is at my side as soon as Uncle Jack pulls away. "You OK?" he whispers, flashing me a grave look.

I nod.

He taps his sneaker against mine, glancing once more at Abigail. "I'll text you later, Parker."

I don't want him to leave, but I offer a small wave as he heads for the door. "Bye, Mike."

Grandma Jane turns to Uncle Jack. "You be careful driving. Lots of wild things out there at night."

Uncle Jack pretends to howl like a wolf, and Grandma Jane gives him a kiss on the cheek. I move toward the window in the living room and watch Uncle Jack walk Abigail across the street. They kiss goodbye, and then he heads for his truck, which is parked in her driveway.

Then Abigail's eyes meet mine, and a shadow seems to lift from her skin and dart toward me. Gasping, I duck, trying to slow down my breaths. The lights flicker with menace.

"Quinn, honey," Mom calls from the kitchen. "Come help me with the dishes."

"Coming," I call back, trying to keep my voice even.

I gather my courage and peek through the window once again; Abigail is gone, but the coldness remains. Shivering, I make my way to the dining room to collect the dessert plates. There, I find Billy lying beneath Abigail's empty chair, lapping up the food she didn't eat. She must have hid it in a napkin and dropped it underneath the table when no one was looking!

"Here, boy," I tell him, trying to coax him away from what's left of the sponge cake.

The lights flicker once more, leaving Billy and me surrounded by shadows. Billy growls with frosting on his lips.

"*Quinn!*" Mom calls again.

With this, the lights return to normal. The shadows melt into the walls, disappearing. Billy and I exchange worried glances before running to join Mom in the kitchen.

CHAPTER 13

Both Mike and I are too tired for our Monday morning run, so I don't see him again until the walk to school.

Something seems to have shifted between us: we walk closer together, my pinky grazing against his thumb so that we're almost holding hands. My stomach twists and turns, but for once, it's actually a good feeling. An excited feeling. Not just fear.

He clears his throat. "So about our mission."

His words seem to knock the magic out of the air. I move my hand away from his and instead grip the straps of my backpack. "The mission, right . . ."

"What's our new plan?"

I look at him. "I honestly don't know anymore."

"Should we warn Lex?"

I shake my head. "She won't believe us. She's under Abigail's spell, remember?"

"What about Mrs. Vega?"

"And say what? That her daughter has joined a ghost cult?"

Mike laughs. "Ghost cult? Good one."

I frown at him. "Be serious."

"I am serious, Parker. I don't know what else to do."

"Me either."

We walk in silence for a little while, kicking a stone between us until I accidentally boot it across the street. Mike raises an eyebrow. "We'll figure it out. We always do."

"I hope so," I mumble as we reach the school.

He sighs. "Maybe we should take the night off from the investigation. You know, try and clear our heads?"

"But what if we're running out of time?"

"Check in with Lex today. See if she'll hang out with you guys after practice or something."

"That's actually not a bad idea."

He grins. "Because I'm—"

"Don't say it!"

"Batman!"

With this, he flips the end of my ponytail and heads into the building. I trudge behind, heading to my locker, where Zoe is already waiting for me.

"Morning," she says with a smile.

"Morning," I tell her, spinning my combination.

She looks at me, no doubt taking in my tired eyes and messy ponytail. "You OK, Quinnie?"

I hover with my fingers on my locker. "It's just Lex," I admit.

Zoe bites her lip. "Yeah, I called her last night to ask her to help me with my language arts homework, and she didn't even pick up. It's like she doesn't want to be our friend anymore." She steps closer to me, dropping her voice. "You don't think that's true, do you? That she doesn't want to be our friend anymore?"

My heart sinks with the thought. For a second, I want to spill the truth to Zoe—to tell her exactly what's been going on and the danger that Lex is in. But what if she doesn't believe me? Or worse, what if telling her makes Zoe another target of the Ladies in White?

"I think we just need a hangout," I tell her. "You know, like at Harvey's or something."

Zoe's eyes light up. "Yes! Quinnie, oh my gosh, that's the best idea ever. She said yes?"

"Well, I haven't asked her yet."

Her face falls. "Oh."

"But I will!" I promise. "In homeroom. She'll say yes. Trust me." I flash her my most reassuring smile, hoping that it looks convincing.

The bell rings above us, scattering kids like ants throughout the hallway. "Don't worry," I say, slamming my locker closed. "See you at lunch!"

I spin into Mr. Feagin's room and find Lex already seated at her desk, her attention focused out the window at the gray morning sky.

"Hey," I say, slipping into the chair beside her.

She barely looks up. "Hey."

"How was your weekend?"

"What?"

"Your weekend," I continue. "Did you do anything fun?"

Lex absently rubs her arms, as if trying to get warm. "It was OK."

"Did you lose power?"

"Not for long."

"Yeah, we only lost it for a few hours."

"I know. Abigail told me."

I blink at her. "Did you work yesterday?"

She sighs. "No. My mom wouldn't let me. We got into a fight about it—she thinks that I'm spending too much time over there. It's not fair. She's spending all of her time with the twins like it's no big deal. Sometimes, it feels like I can never make her happy."

I notice the way that Lex's eyes darken as she talks about her mom. Abigail must be instigating some of these thoughts. Mrs. Vega and Lex have always been so close—close to the point that Zoe, Kaylee, and I used to envy their relationship. If Abigail's endgame is to make Lex willingly give up her family, this has to be part of the diabolical plan.

"Your mom probably just misses you," I say. "We all kind of do. I can't remember the last time we hung out."

"It's not just *my* fault," she shoots back defensively. "You and Kaylee are always at track, Zoe babysits after school or has piano lessons—"

I hold up my hand to cut her off. "I'm not blaming you, Lex. I just think it would be cool if we could all hang out again. You know, like normal."

Before she can answer, Mr. Feagin stands up and clears his throat. "Hey, folks, quick announcement," he says, straightening his glasses. "I just got an e-mail saying that all after-school activities are canceled today for storm cleanup. That includes all sports, even indoor ones."

I don't know whether to be grateful or frustrated, because I still need to redeem myself on the field. I guess it could be worse: now at least the girls and I can get to Harvey's sooner rather than later.

The bell rings, and Lex jumps to her feet, rushing for the door. I chase after her.

"What about this afternoon?" I ask. "We meet you at your locker after school and all walk over to Harvey's together."

Kids push past us as Lex and I hover in the doorframe. Her jaw is set, as if she's about to shoot me down.

"Please," I beg, bringing my voice down to just above a whisper. "I think we all need this."

Lex's face softens. "OK," she finally says. "I guess one milkshake won't hurt."

"Ladies, let's move along to class," Mr. Feagin says before I can answer.

Lex gives a small wave before hurrying down the hallway. I break off in the opposite direction.

"I'll believe it when I see it," Zoe mutters when I tell her about it later in Spanish. "I doubt she's going to show."

"Stop being so pessimistic," I urge. "She seemed sincere."

Zoe rolls her eyes. "Whatever. We'll see."

A part of me doesn't believe it either, and by the time lunch rolls around, I'm half-expecting her to bail. For the entire half hour, I'm sitting on the edge of my bench, ready for her to make up an excuse, or to throw out Abigail's name, or something. But she just picks at her lunch quietly with a vacant expression on her face.

When the bell rings, she stands up, tucks her lunchbox under her arm, and says, "See you after school."

Zoe's jaw drops. "You're actually coming?"

Lex's eyebrows narrow. "Why wouldn't I? You invited me."

"Yeah, but I didn't think you'd show."

"Your locker," I cut in quickly, flashing Zoe a look. "We'll meet you at your locker after school, and we can all walk to Harvey's together."

Lex takes a deep breath, almost as if she's about to turn us down again, but loses the nerve. "OK. See you later." She floats away, leaving Zoe, Kaylee, and me behind to stare after her.

"You better be nice," Kaylee tells Zoe, nudging her arm.

Zoe feigns her most innocent look. "Me? I'm always nice."

"Let's go," I mutter, tugging her down the hall to class.

It takes everything I've got just to focus on the work I'm supposed to complete this afternoon: teachers introduce new topics and assignments that I know I need to pay attention to, but I just can't stop thinking about Lex, and the Ladies in White, and the poisonings . . .

A heaviness presses against my chest. *What if Mike and I can't figure this out? What if we fail?*

A closed fist knocks gently on my desk. "Earth to Quinn?" Zoe asks, her eyes narrowed in concern. "You OK?"

I nod as the last bell rings. "Let's go meet Lex and Kaylee."

We gather our things and make our way to Lex's locker, where we find them waiting for us.

Lex smiles at us—something I haven't seen in weeks. "You guys ready? I'm actually kind of dying for a shake. It's been a while since I had one."

"It's been a while for a lot of things," Zoe mutters before I whack her in the arm. She clears her throat and smiles back at Lex. "I'm just kidding. Let's go."

We pass Mike on our way out of Rocky Hill. I give him a little nod, and when the girls aren't looking, I mouth the words *See you later.* He flashes a thumbs-up sign right before my friends and I head onto the sidewalk.

The wind is still heavy in the aftermath of the storm, causing our hair to fly in all directions as we tug our hoodies tighter around us, laughing. The leaves swirl at our feet almost magically, like a dance. Together, we parade down Main Street, recapping our days in a way that feels just like old times. By the time we reach Harvey's, we're back to finishing each other's sentences and talking over one another.

"Can I take your order?" a high school boy asks as he skates over to our table.

We shove our backpacks underneath the booth and rattle off our elaborate milkshake orders. When they arrive, we slurp them down so fast that we get brain freezes. I don't remember the last time I laughed so hard. It makes me feel brand-new. I find myself wishing that this moment will never end, that there will be more days like this, and that the little blip in our friendship was just that—a blip. This hope courses through my bones—until, all of a sudden, a piano trill cuts through all the chatter. A ringtone. We all glance at Lex, as she digs around for her phone.

"Don't answer it," Zoe tells her.

"But it's Abigail."

"How do you know? Does she have her own ringtone?" Zoe cries. "Do *I* have my own ringtone?"

Lex ignores her and looks at her phone, scrolling through the message with an urgency that makes me uneasy. I try to casually steal a glance at her screen, but she guards it in such a way that makes it impossible for me to read anything past the first line: **Where are you?**

I stiffen. "You're not leaving, right?"

Almost instantly, the color washes out of Lex's cheeks, the light lost from her eyes. She's no longer smiling; instead, she looks tired, weighed down.

"I have to," she says quietly. "I'm already late."

"But we haven't even been here that long," Kaylee points out. "We just ordered a second shake to share."

"You guys can split it," Lex says, gathering her things from underneath the table and tugging on her white hoodie. "I'm full anyways."

"Lex, wait," I start, but she's already waving me off.

"I'm sorry. I have to go." There is a hint of regret and sorrow in her eyes. She's clearly conflicted about leaving us for Abigail.

There's still time, I realize. *She's not as far gone as it seems.*

"See you," she says.

Our server approaches with our communal milkshake just as Lex walks away. He watches after her, confused.

"You guys still want this?" he asks.

"We'll just take it to go, please," Zoe says, before resting her chin into her hands as if defeated.

"It was fun while it lasted," Kaylee says quietly.

"Stop it," I tell them. "Stop acting like she's gone forever."

Zoe makes a face. "Well, it feels like she is. I mean, that was the first time I saw her smile in who knows how long?"

I shake my head. "She'll be back. As soon as this thing with Abigail ends, she'll be back to her old self. I know it."

"But Lex isn't going to quit volunteering—she loves it. She lives for it." Zoe arches an eyebrow. "Unless you have some kind of master plan that we don't know about? Some way to lure Lex away from Abigail?"

I can't help but think how right Zoe is about this. "Maybe." I put my money on the table. "But in the meantime, I should get home."

"Ugh. I guess that means I have to go babysit soon."

"Guess so."

We pay our bill, tip the server, and head out onto the sidewalk. The sun warms the cobblestones beneath our feet as the wind starts to settle.

"See you tomorrow," we tell one another, before breaking off in opposite directions.

At home, I notice a text from Mike: ***Can't plan tonight. Big Mandarin test in the morning. Gotta study.***

OK, I write back. **We can pick up the investigation tomorrow.**

I don't know if I feel relief or disappointment as I drop my phone onto the table next to a note from Mom saying that she's working late.

"It's just you and me," I tell Billy, before digging out some of Grandma Jane's leftovers from the fridge.

I eat in front of the TV with Billy on the couch next to me. I try to focus on the show, but my mind keeps fluttering between images: Zoe's worried eyes, Lex's empty smile, Abigail's threatening grip on my shoulder.

Mrs. Hudson had said we can't stop the Ladies in White. But if there's a way for a ghost to linger in the human world, there must be a way to get them out.

Billy rests his head on my lap. He smells like Grandma Jane's oils, and I think tonight would be a good night to try a cup of tea. Before bed, I brew myself a mug, and for the first time in days, I fall asleep easily. I dream about Abigail, about her ghostly face turning translucent, exposing her for what she really is. Then her teeth turn to fangs, her fingers morph into claws, and she lunges at me. I wake with a start, blinking my room into focus.

I'm alone. I'm safe.

The darkness is that heavy, dead-of-night type, the type that tricks you into seeing shapes and shadows and other things that seem to move but shouldn't. *It's nothing*, I try to convince myself, before I settle back, slowing down my breaths and forcing my eyes to close.

"Quinn..."

I jolt forward in the bed again, gasping. In the corner by the window stands my dad—not a swirling, misty version of his face, but my actual, moving, smiling dad. Then his body flickers like a light bulb that needs to be changed. He's dressed in the same outfit that he's wearing in the photo on my dresser: a T-shirt and a pair of running shorts that exposes the Florida-shaped scar on the back of his calf. I can make out the birthmarks, the freckles, the laugh lines, the stubble on his chin. The only thing that's missing is the color. Instead of shades of brown and blue, Dad's skin and clothes are all shades of gray. Like a black-and-white photograph come to life.

"Quinn," he says again, his voice coming through in a whisper. A shadow hovers behind him like black wings that rise and fall as he moves to the door. The lights flicker on and off in a sporadic rhythm that matches the uneven beats of my heart. In an instant, his entire body seeps through the wood, disappearing right in front of me.

"Dad—wait!"

I scramble from the bed, practically falling through the door into the hallway.

He stops at the top of the stairs and puts a finger to his

lips and makes a pointed look toward my mother's bedroom. *"Shh!"*

He then glides down the stairs, the wings spread out behind him. As quietly as possible, I follow him all the way to the front door. Once again, he beckons me forward, before seeping through the wood. I know that he's waiting for me outside, ready to lead me who knows where. I hesitate with my hand on the knob, my heart beating so fast that I'm afraid the sound will wake up Billy upstairs. Or Mom.

Mike's face suddenly pops into my mind, and I remember what he said during our fight earlier: *It's not really your dad. It could be a demon tricking you. It could be Abigail.*

My hands and feet feel cold and tingly. I can hear my dad call to me from the porch, begging me to follow.

But what if Mike's right? What if this is a trick?

It doesn't matter. I need to know.

I turn the handle and push through. The air outside is thick and raw from the leftover rain. My dad is waiting for me on the sidewalk. He nods his head toward the end of the cul-de-sac, in the direction of the pond. My stomach turns and the balls of my feet start to itch, daring me to run away. Instead, I nod. I follow.

"Parker!"

I spin around, gasping as Mike races toward me.

"What are you doing here?" I hiss, making sure to keep my voice down on the otherwise silent street.

"I saw you from my window."

"Why were you watching me from your window?"

"I can't sleep, remember? Anyway, who cares? What are *you* doing, Parker?"

I bristle at his tone. "Talking to my dad." I jut my chin toward the edge of the cul-de-sac, where my dad's body flashes like a firefly before it disappears through the trees.

"Oh my—"

"You see him, don't you?"

"Of course I see him! But that doesn't mean we should follow him—hey, wait. Parker! Park-er!"

I'm already gone, taking off down the street. I can hear Mike's whisper-yells and footsteps behind me as we break through the woods, which still look mangled by the weekend storm. I hadn't thought that it was possible for the pond to look any creepier than it already did, but the fallen branches piercing through the water cast extra shadows around the embankment.

Dad stays ahead of us, hovering at the edge of the pond beside the lightning tree. Then the bark seems to absorb Dad's light and starts to glow. Water begins spilling over the stone wall at the pond's edge, spreading out over the muck and the pond grass, all the way down to the back artery of side streets—the ones farthest from Goodie Lane.

"*Quinn,*" Dad says again, only this time his voice sounds different—higher than it should be.

"Dad, what—"

I get as close as I can before Mike grabs my arm, pulling me back. "You can talk to it from over here," he tells me, not shifting his eyes away from my dad.

The flickering intensifies, distorting his gray face and features. Mike squeezes my bicep, trying to pull me away. I stand firm.

"Dad?"

Only it's not my dad anymore. It's a woman with wide hollow eyes. It's Cami! Her body is draped in a long white dress that makes it seem as though she's floating. Her hair is hanging loose around her shoulders, and the closer she gets, the more taken I am with just how young she looks.

"Cami? But—what?" I can feel the tears burning my eyes as I realize that Mike was right. My dad never came back to me.

"I'm sorry for tricking you," she says, moving until she's standing directly in front of us. "I had to get you here."

"Ever think of *asking*?" Mike snarls. "Seriously, do you realize how messed up that was? Making her think that her dad was . . ." He trails off, not wanting to say the thing that I'm already thinking. *Making me think that my dad was back.*

"I didn't think you'd come if you knew it was me," Cami says, and her voice sounds far away and broken, crackling like static.

"That's such a load of—"

"What do you *want*?" I cry, my limbs shaking so fiercely that I half-expect sparks to fly from my fingertips.

"I can't stay," she says, her words blending with the wind. "But I had to warn you."

Mike waves her off. "We already know about you and your ghost sisters. About *Abigail*."

Cami's eyes widen, and for a second they look empty, like two holes carved into white stone. "What do you *think* you know?"

"That Abigail killed you. Poison. Along with the other ones," Mike continues, spitting out the words. "And we know about Abigail's *real* daughters, the ones who died."

I tug hard on his arm, suddenly nervous. He's telling her too much.

"You know *nothing*!" Cami yells, the static in her voice so piercing that Mike and I fall to the ground, covering our ears.

Winged shadows stretch and swim around the trees, dancing with a menace that makes me huddle closer to Mike.

"It was you!" I realize, shouting through the wind. "You've been the shadows. You were in my kitchen—you—you . . ." I trail off and bend over, feeling faint and nauseous. Mike puts his arms around me and squeezes.

The wind settles, and the shadows seem to sink into the pond. Cami's feet return to earth, and she looks at me for the first time with what seems like sympathy. I force myself to stand, squaring myself off against her.

"Why are you here?" I ask, staring hard at her hollow eyes. "What do you want?"

"I came to warn you," she says, playing with the hem of her dress. "You have to save your friend."

"Lex?"

She grimaces at the mention of Lex's name. "She's getting too close to Abigail. I was supposed to be the *last* one. She promised." There's something in her eyes that look so sad and soft: for a second, I can see the girl she once was. The girl she should have been.

"Last one, what?" Mike asks, joining my side. "Ghost daughter?" He snorts. "Don't you know how cults work? There's never a *last* one."

Cami glares at him. I feel the wind pick up in my hair, and I step in front of Mike.

"He doesn't mean that," I say. "Please. Finish what you were saying."

It takes forever for Cami's gaze to shift back to mine, but when it does, the air around us settles.

"She saved me, you know," she finally says, her voice softer. Her eyes look far away now, as if she's remembering something. "I didn't have a mother like you two. Neither did my sisters. Abigail gave us a new life. She brought us together and made us the family of our dreams."

"Yeah, by *poisoning* you," Mike mutters.

"Is that the plan?" I ask Cami. "Is Abigail going to poison Lex?" My heart races with the question.

"That's why I'm here."

I gasp. "When?"

"Tomorrow night. Where Abigail was once buried."

"The cemetery?" Mike balks.

"But how do we stop her?" I ask, instinctively gripping Mike's hand to keep my own fingers from trembling.

Color flickers across Cami's cheeks, settling into a sad, pale blue. "Abigail has to *want* to cross over. And from what she's said, the only reason she would consider it would be if she found her girls—her original girls."

"Yeah, about that," Mike starts, pulling out his phone and showing the photo of the graves to Cami.

"It's Christopher!" she says. "You found him! He's at Unity after all?"

Mike and I exchange looks before he answers, "Sort of."

Cami's smile quickly fades. "What do you mean?" She studies the picture again, leaning in to make sure she hasn't missed any other grave markers.

"Abigail's not there," he says, his voice shaking as he starts to explain, tucking his phone into his pocket. "She's not buried with her kids."

"What? No," Cami says, shaking her head. "You've got this wrong. Abigail *is* there—I've seen the plot."

"Her grave is at Unity," I interrupt, "but Christopher's and the girls' are across the street."

Cami's eyes widen. "I don't understand."

I hesitate, wondering how dangerous it is to tell her what we know. *Can we trust a ghost? Right now, she looks human. And she* did *bring us here to warn us about Abigail. Can she really help us?* I take a deep breath. *There's only one way to find out.*

"Christopher is buried in his backyard," I tell her. "He bought the house across the street, the one that overlooks the cemetery."

"The old woman?" Cami asks.

Mike nods. "She was his second wife. He probably wanted to be closer to his daughters."

"But at some point," I continue, "Christopher had the girls' graves moved. The three of them are buried by the woods behind his house, but Abigail's still at Unity."

It's as if Cami's face has suddenly become a prism: every color imaginable flashes over her translucent skin as she processes what we just told her. I take a step back, sticking close to Mike as I pull myself onto the balls of my feet, ready to run if need be.

"I can't believe he left her," Cami cries, her voice causing tiny ripples to skirt across the pond. "What kind of person moves a mother's daughters away from her? Now Abigail will never be at peace! Don't you get it? She's not going to stop. She's going to harvest more souls after Lex. She may even try to take a partner."

Mike and I gasp. "Uncle Jack?"

Cami nods.

I take a defiant step toward her, my fists still clenched at my side. I'm so close to her that it feels as though I'm stepping into a walk-in freezer, but I don't care. "I'm going to stop her if it's the last thing I do."

We stand off against each other until Mike tugs me back by the arm, the warmth from his fingertips melting some of Cami's ice.

Eventually, Cami bows her head. "I want to help you."

"Yeah, right," Mike breathes. "Like you'd ever turn against your ghost mother."

"I do love Abigail," Cami admits, her skin flickering once again. "But I'm starting to think that my sisters and I will never be enough for her. I was supposed to be the last soul. And with Lex—it just doesn't seem right. She comes from a good home. A good mother . . ." Cami trails off, looking weighed down by sadness.

"So what do we do?" I ask.

"We have to bring her to the other graves. Tomorrow night. Before she—"

"Before she kills my friend," I finish.

Her eyelashes flutter. "Yes."

"But if you help us, then won't you pass over, too?" Mike asks. "Won't you all pass over?"

Cami nods, and Mike turns to me. "We can't trust her, Parker. She's a liar. It could all be a trap. She loves Abigail—she admitted it! Why would she give up her ghost life just to help some kid she barely knows?"

"What other choice do we have?" I ask.

For a moment, it looks as if Mike might continue to argue, but instead he sighs and looks at Cami. "You better not be tricking us again," he tells her, puffing out his chest as though he isn't scared to threaten a dangerous ghost.

"No more tricks," she promises, fading into the darkness. "My sisters and I will be there tomorrow. Find us at Abigail's resting place. Nine o'clock. I'll talk to my sisters, and we'll try lure her toward the other graves." She shrugs. "Hopefully, it's enough." With this, her whole body turns translucent, until all that's left is a shadow.

I realize that I'm still holding Mike's hand, but I don't dare let go. We look at each other for a moment before taking off, bolting toward Goodie Lane.

We don't even say goodbye before sneaking back into our houses, but as soon as I'm safe inside my room, I text him. He calls back immediately.

"Parker," he whispers, keeping his voice low.

"Hey, Mike." I kick off my shoes and fall onto my bed. "We need a plan."

"I think we should tell Mrs. Vega," he says.

"We can't," I tell him.

"We have to, Parker. This is too dangerous. It's way bigger than us. Lex can get killed."

"You think I don't know that?" I feel the frustration spreading through my body. "We can't go to Mrs. Vega. Worst-case scenario, she won't believe us and we're still alone. Best-case scenario, she believes us and goes to the police. Meanwhile, Abigail disappears."

"But maybe she'd disappear *before* hurting Lex."

"Were you listening to the same conversation as me?" I hiss. "Abigail has murdered four people that we know of. Cami and Mrs. Hudson both said that Abigail is *unstoppable*. Besides, if she doesn't get Lex, it'll be another girl in another town!"

"If she's so unstoppable, then how are we supposed to save Lex all by ourselves?" Mike counters.

"Because we won't *be* by ourselves, Mike. The other Ladies in White are on our side."

I hear him sigh loudly into the phone. "Parker, do you really believe Cami?"

My heart beats faster as I stare at the shadows on the walls, my fingers clasping Grandma Jane's crystal. "Yes," I tell him, remembering the humanity shining through her dead eyes. "And I think that once Abigail sees her daughters' graves—"

"That she'll forget about Lex?" Mike finishes. "And we can get her out of there?"

"Yes."

We sit in silence for a moment. My eyes linger on Dad's photograph on my dresser—the one that Cami must have used to impersonate him. *He never came back.* The realization causes my throat to tighten. Tears spill down my cheeks, and I sniffle.

"Parker? Are you OK?" His voice is soft. Gentle. I can picture his brows pinched together with concern.

"I'm fine," I lie, swiping away my tears. "Let's just figure out our plan."

"I mean, there's not much *to* plan. Cami said that if we meet them at the graveyard tomorrow night, then she'll help us lure Abigail to her daughters' graves."

"So am I just supposed to act like everything is normal tomorrow at school?" I ask, raising my voice a little louder than I mean to.

"Hey, you're the one who wants to trust Ghost Girl," Mike tells me. "If we're going with Cami's plan, then yeah, you have to fake a smile tomorrow. At least until the cemetery."

"We should be early," I say. "You know, to Unity. I want to be there to follow them as soon as they cross the gate."

"Agreed."

I hear him yawn. "Go to bed, Mike. We need our rest for tomorrow."

"I'm not tired," he says through a second yawn.

"You need your beauty sleep. Good *night!*"

He laughs softly. "Night, Parker."

With this, we both hang up, and I fall down against my pillow, pulling the covers up to my chin. The darkness in the space feels heavier without Mike on the line. Part of me has the urge to call him back, but hopefully he's already sleeping.

Seriously, though, how am I supposed to close my eyes when there is a monster plotting to kill my friend tomorrow night?

I try to text Lex, but as usual, there's no response. My fingers shake as they type, writing her message after message, before giving up and plugging in my phone.

The weight of each second ticks in my chest as the sky outside my window grows lighter. I don't know how many minutes or hours tick by before Billy nudges his way into my room, hopping onto my bed.

"Hey, you," I whisper, pulling his sweet face toward mine. He licks my cheek and curls up next to me, letting out a low, contented sigh. And finally, with Billy nuzzled against me, I find sleep.

CHAPTER 14

I sleep straight through our run, and for once I don't care. I'm so tired that my bones hurt. Billy growls at my alarm clock before slumping back down onto the bed.

"I feel you, boy."

He watches me through heavy lids as I flit around the room, dressing in yet another shirt that had been gifted to me by Lex. I tuck Grandma Jane's crystal in my pocket, before spritzing on some of her lavender oil.

"Come on, Billy."

Grudgingly, he follows me downstairs, where Mom waits in the kitchen.

"Morning, sweetie," she says with a smile, running a hand through the end of my ponytail. "Did you sleep OK?"

I shrug, and she raises a concerned eyebrow. "What's up, honey? You feel all right?" She presses the back of her hand against my forehead, inspecting me for a fever.

"I'm fine," I tell her. "I just—I don't know—couldn't get comfortable last night."

"You can always come get me if that happens, you know?"

"I know."

She drains the rest of her coffee before dropping the mug in the sink. "Come on," she says. "I can give you and Michael a ride. I don't have to be at work until later this afternoon."

"Are you working late tonight?" I ask, thinking about our mission at the cemetery.

"I should be home around twelve." Her face softens. "Sorry, honey. We'll have dinner tomorrow night, OK? Go and get your stuff."

Billy follows me to the living room, where I grab my coat and bag, pulling the straps over my shoulders. Mom hands me a granola bar, and together we head outside.

Mike is waiting in the driveway, looking as tired as I feel. His eyes widen when he notices my mom.

"Morning, Mrs. Parker," he says politely, his voice sounding ragged from what I can only assume is lack of sleep.

"Hi, Michael. How you doing?"

"I'm good."

"Mom's giving us a ride this morning," I tell him.

He follows us to the car and climbs in the backseat. I sit in the front next to Mom, and she cranks the radio as we head to school. She sings, staying surprisingly on-key, until we reach the drop-off circle.

"Have a good day," she says. "And Quinnie, text me when you get home. There's still some of Grandma Jane's leftovers in the fridge."

"OK."

"Thanks for the ride, Mrs. Parker," Mike says, waiting for me on the sidewalk.

"Bye, Mom. Love you." The words catch in my throat, and I hope that Mike doesn't notice.

"Love you, too, Starshine. I'll check on you when I get home."

With this, I close my door and give her one last wave from the sidewalk. My heart beats faster as I watch her drive away. Mike loops his hand in mine and gives it a squeeze, before letting it drop back down at my side.

"Did you sleep last night?" he asks as we slowly make our way inside.

"Nope. You?"

"Nope."

"Why didn't you text me?" I ask.

"I didn't want to wake you in case *you* were sleeping." He points to his chest. "I'm a thoughtful guy, Parker."

"Well, if you're so thoughtful, what were you thinking about all night?"

"Our mission, obviously. We just have to keep a low profile," he says, pushing through the double doors. "You know, keep our heads down and act like everything is normal until tonight. Then, we act fast."

"*Very* fast."

We stop at the end of the hallway when we see Lex. Her long, thin arms heave a pile of books into her locker. She looks frail, almost as if her limbs will snap if she lifts anything else.

"Don't worry," Mike whispers, bringing his face close to mine. "We're going to save her. These ghost ladies have *nothing* on the Oldies. And we vanquished them like *that*." He snaps his fingers.

He kind of has a point, and I feel my shoulders relax slightly.

"Just stay with her as much as possible," he tells me. "See what you can find out—if she mentions anything about tonight."

I nod. "I'm on it."

He smiles. "And for the record, Parker, there's no one I'd rather go into ghost battle with than you."

I feel my cheeks redden as he saunters away. I take a deep breath and head over toward Lex.

"Morning," I say, trying to make my voice sound as light as possible. "Your hair looks pretty today."

"Thanks," she mumbles, barely looking at me as she slams her locker closed. She spins on her heels, making her way to homeroom without me.

I follow her after I dump my stuff in my own locker. Mr. Feagin is talking to Lex from behind his desk, his eyes narrowed through his glasses.

"Are you feeling all right? You seem a bit tired. I can write you a pass to the nurse if you want."

"I'm fine, Mr. Feagin."

"Are you sure? It's no trouble, I can just—"

"I said I'm fine."

She turns and stomps off toward her desk without another look at our baffled teacher. I drop into the seat next to her.

Mr. Feagin's not wrong. Lex's healthy skin tone has faded to a sickly shade that appears lost in her loose white clothes. I can see the bones in her shoulder blades as she hunches over the desk. She's always slouching lately, as if she doesn't have the energy to hold herself up.

"Lex," I start, but the words freeze on my tongue when she turns to me. For a second, I don't recognize her: her high cheekbones seem to jut out more than usual, causing her face to look sunken, almost skeletal. Her large eyes look bulbous, with dark circles aging her about a decade.

"What?" she asks.

"I—I ..."

"*What*, Quinn?"

"Never mind. Sorry."

The bell rings, and I rush out of the room as fast as I can manage without tripping over myself. Booking it around the corner, I slam right into Zoe.

"Jeez, Quinnie! Watch where you're going."

"Sorry." I bend down to help her retrieve her dropped binder. "I just didn't want to be late."

"It's cool. The bell hasn't even rung yet for first period."

We stand back up and walk to Spanish class together, elbow to elbow.

"So, I was thinking," Zoe starts, her voice bright and excited. "We are in desperate need of a movie night."

"What, like *now*?"

"Not *now*, now. But maybe Saturday. We haven't had one since the summer. That's ridiculous! We used to have them every weekend."

"Yeah, but remember how hard it was just getting everyone to Harvey's last week?"

She raises a brow. "And by *everyone* you mean Lex, right?"

"Well, yeah," I say, my stomach turning.

She waves a hand. "Don't worry about her. She'll come."

"How can you be so sure?"

"Because she had fun at Harvey's. You saw her—she laughed, she talked, she drank a freaking milkshake,

Quinnie! Other than that, when was the last time you saw that girl eat or drink anything?"

I shrug, not wanting to answer.

"Just leave it to me. This Saturday night—I'll get Lex to come. I mean, who can resist this face?" Zoe asks, pointing to her own exaggerated grin. "Besides, Halloween is coming up. When has Lex ever turned down a themed night? We can watch bad horror movies and eat candy corn. It'll be like old times."

What I'd give for things to be like "old times" again...

"I'll tell her she can pick our costumes for Halloween," Zoe continues. "She's always been wanting to do a group thing."

"Yeah, and *you* always shoot her down," I point out.

"Well, not anymore! I'll give her total creative control. Maybe we can still try and get Marion Jones to do our makeup? Lex has been dying to get on Marion's list since sixth grade."

It's unlikely, but if we *could* get Marion, Lex would be so into it. "Maybe," I say. "I mean, we can try."

We slide into Spanish class just as the bell rings.

I feel like I'm floating through the rest of my morning classes, my feet not quite hitting the ground. *Maybe I'm turning into a ghost myself.* The idea makes me shudder.

Everyone's already at the lunch table by the time I get to the cafeteria.

"Hey, guys," I say, joining them.

"We were just talking about the sleepover," Zoe tells me.

"Halloween candy and movies? I'm in," Kaylee says through a mouthful of salad.

"Me too," I say, unzipping my lunch bag. I pull out a cheese-and-pickle sandwich and a packet of kettle chips. I tear off a corner of bread and nibble it as I study Lex. She seems to be in another world, her large eyes staring at an invisible spot on the table as her lunch sits unopened in front of her.

"What about you?" Zoe asks. "You in, Lex?" Her voice sounds so hopeful that it breaks my heart. "We can talk about costumes. We thought it could be cool if you chose a group costume for us all to wear on Halloween. Right, guys?"

"Of course, yeah," Kaylee and I say.

It takes Lex so long to answer that for a moment I don't think that she's even heard us. "I don't know," she finally says, still not looking at us. "I'll have to ask Abigail."

Zoe's jaw sets with determination. "I talked to Marion Jones last period. She's going to put us on her makeup list. Isn't that awesome?"

We all hold our breaths, waiting for Lex to scream with excitement. Nothing.

"Lex? Did you hear me?" Zoe asks. She motions toward the table in the back corner of the cafeteria where Marion sits, digging into her metal Count Chocula lunch box. Her black hair is pulled into two buns on the top of her head, and she keeps her head down as she eats. She looks shy—you'd never guess that come Halloween, she's the most popular kid at school.

"Lex!"

"I said I'd *think* about it," Lex growls.

We sit in silence for a moment. I suddenly feel too sick to eat. Mike catches my eye at the next table, and I shoot back a worried look. His voice pops into my head: *See if she mentions anything about tonight.*

"How's it going at Abigail's?" I ask, trying to keep my voice as casual as possible. "You still like it?"

She brightens with the mention of Abigail's name. *"Great,"* she gushes, stretching out the word into multiple syllables. "We just closed a big account in New Haven. Abigail is going to take us all out to celebrate tonight."

My ears perk up. "Tonight?"

"Yup. I already picked out my outfit. I'm so excited."

Zoe, Kaylee, and I exchange looks, but Lex doesn't seem to notice.

"Where are you going?" I ask.

Zoe snorts. "Probably not Cucina Della Nonna's. I bet Abigail is too much of a snob to eat pizza."

"She's not a snob, she's classy!" Lex counters, becoming animated for the first time all period. "Besides, I don't know where we're going. It's a surprise."

"But what if you don't like it?" I ask, gripping the edge of my lunch bag.

"I trust Abigail," Lex says matter-of-factly.

You shouldn't.

"Well, when you're done pretending that you're a design student, maybe you can hang out with your *real* friends every once in a while," Zoe mutters.

Lex just blinks at her as the bell rings. Without another word, Zoe storms off with Kaylee trailing behind, leaving me alone with Lex. I try to keep the conversation going as we collect our things.

"Is your mom cool with you going out with Abigail on a school night?" I ask.

She shrugs one shoulder as if she hadn't even thought about it. "She's busy with the twins. Rehearsals every night until late. And when she comes home, she finishes her work in the kitchen."

"But doesn't she know that you're gone?" I press. "Like when you stay overnight at Abigail's?"

A wicked smile spreads across her face. "She doesn't know. I text her to say that I'm asleep so that she doesn't knock on my door when she comes home. Then I'm back in the morning before she even notices that I was gone."

I can't help myself. "That's kind of messed up, Lex."

The smile disappears in a flash. "Who are *you* to judge?"

"I'm just worried about you."

"Stop saying that!" she cries, turning heads as people mill out of the cafeteria.

"Lex, I'm sorry—"

"None of you ever support me," she continues, the rage making her shake as she grips the handle of her lunch box. "You know what, Quinn? Forget it. I'm *done*."

"Lex, wait!"

But she storms off into the crowded hallway, vanishing in the sea of students.

Mike walks over. "So that went well."

I feel my heart sink even lower in my chest. "We can't mess up tonight."

"We won't mess up."

The second bell rings around us, and we race off to our next class.

By the time I get to track practice after school, my legs are burning to run. I know this team isn't as important as, you know, saving your best friend's life from a poltergeist. But being on this field feels *right*. It's like there's gunpowder in my shoes, ready to shoot me straight across the finish line. I start to imagine that I'm being chased by shadows, their dark heads eyeless and full of teeth that snap behind my legs. I launch forward, trying to outrun the cold and reach the warmth.

"Attagirl, Parker!" Coach cries, clapping. "Way to hustle.

Now *that*," he starts, spinning around to face my teammates, "is how you run the 400 dash."

I catch my breath as Kaylee high-fives me on the sidelines, and, to my surprise, so does Jess. Then Coach calls up the boys. Mike's in this heat. I take a large drag of water as I watch him line up. Coach blows his whistle, and the boys spring into action, their legs graceful as they fly forward. Mike should be first—Mike's always first—but he's falling behind. He looks tired. He looks like he's run twelve miles instead of 400 meters.

He ends up coming in dead last.

"Warren! Get over here!" Coach barks.

I jump at the sound of Mike's last name: Coach never has to yell at Mike. Mike's head is hung low as he bites his bottom lip.

He starts listing everything Mike did wrong. "Lack of focus . . . running like you're half-asleep . . ." Coach goes on and on. Mike's teammates gawk until the tirade is over. When Coach notices that the other boys have just been standing around, he orders them all to do push-ups. We girls are allowed to change.

I wait at the bottom of the hill for a sorry-looking Mike, who eventually joins me by the fence.

"Hey," he mutters, tugging his hat down low.

I give him a half-hearted smile. "Come on. Let's get out of here."

We trudge in time to each other without saying anything until we land on Goodie Lane.

"Are you sure you're OK?" I ask when we get to his house.

"I'm fine," he insists, puffing out his chest, trying his best to convince me. But no matter how low he pulls down his hat, I can still see the pain and worry in his eyes.

I take his hand and squeeze. My heart pounds as I wait for him to squeeze back. It seems to take forever, but finally he does. His fingers feel soft and warm. I don't want to let go.

"Talk to me," I urge.

"I just . . . It's just . . ." He searches for the right words. "Parker, it's a lot. I'm still dreaming about the Oldies, and now we have to fight Oldies 2.0, and I don't feel ready."

"That makes sense," I tell him. "I mean, when would you *ever* really feel ready to go into ghost battle? But I'll be there." I force a small smile. "We make a great team, Mike. And I wouldn't have been able to vanquish the Oldies without you."

He snorts, his expression becoming more animated. "That's true. You would've been fish food in that dirty pond if it weren't for me."

"Yeah, yeah. You *technically* saved my life." I wave him off.

He tilts up the brim of his hat and looks at me. "Cause I'm Batman, right? Don't try to deny it."

I laugh, and he laughs, and for a second everything feels so blissfully normal.

"We do make a good team, don't we, Parker?"

"The best. You know we got this, Mike."

"Yeah. We got this because I got you."

I feel my cheeks redden, and I have to look away to hide my blush. Before I can fumble a response, his front door swings open. I drop his hand as Mrs. Warren steps outside. She smiles at us.

"I thought I heard you," she says. "You kids hungry? I've got plenty of lasagna. Quinn, do you want to stay for dinner?"

"Thanks, Mrs. Warren, but I have to go feed Billy."

"OK. You know where we are if you change your mind." She turns back in to the house.

I look at Mike. "Is that cool? Or do you need me to stay?"

"Yeah, I'm cool now. Go get Billy. Give him a biscuit for me."

Just as I start to back away, Mike pulls me toward him for a hug, and before I know what's happening, my arms wrap around his waist. We stay like this for who knows how long, with the breeze running through the end of my ponytail, his palms pressed against my back, and our toes touching through our sneakers. I breathe in the fabric of his T-shirt as my head rests against his shoulder. When we pull away, I feel stronger.

He smiles and tilts his hat back down. "Later, Parker."

I offer him a soft smile. "I'll see you at eight thirty." With this, I cut across our driveways and let myself inside, my limbs still feeling like Jell-O.

Billy greets me at the door, trotting in small half-circles as he wags his tail.

"Hi, boy." I ruffle his fur a bit before letting him out to do his business. When he comes back in, I make myself a sandwich and give Billy a fresh bowl of kibble.

"Eat up," I tell him.

Even though I need all my strength for tonight, the food feels wrong in my stomach, and eventually I just push the sandwich away unfinished. Instead, I watch Billy as he blissfully devours his own dinner. After one last lick, his eyes meet mine, and he lets out a little bark as if to say *thank you.*

"You're welcome," I say, suddenly wishing that I could spend a quiet night on the couch with him.

I throw a glance out of the dark window and I can't help but shiver. *What will tonight bring? Can we really save Lex? Or will this ambush only make Abigail more vengeful and bitter?*

Billy comes up and nudges me in the side of my thigh. It's probably just my imagination, but I swear that for a second, his eyes flicker toward the basement door.

"What's up, boy?"

And there it is again: the slightest twitch, followed by an encouraging bark. Standing up, I motion for him to follow me. Together, we descend the creaky stairs, down into the musky basement. Billy trots ahead, stopping in front of Dad's old filing cabinets. I haven't really been down here since last summer, but for some reason, Billy seems to think there's something important in these drawers. Standing on my tiptoes, I tug open the top one and peer inside. Just files—boring adult paperwork for taxes or whatever.

The second drawer, however, takes my breath away: resting on top of a pile of certificates is Dad's class photo from middle school. He's smiling in that boyish way that makes my heart ache. His brown eyes are warm, and for a moment I swear that I can feel them twinkle. It's almost as if he's breathing through the picture, watching me, telling me that everything's going to be OK.

I hug the photograph to my chest and start crying. Billy rubs his nose against my leg, and I drop to a heap on the concrete floor. Billy curls up in my lap. Here we remain until I hear the familiar *Batman* theme song ringing from the kitchen. Billy cocks his head to the side, barks once, and bolts up the stairs. Taking a deep breath, I snap off the light, following Billy up. I clutch the photograph in one hand while answering my cell phone with the other.

"Hello?"

"Parker, where are you?" Mike gasps. "It's eight thirty!"

My heart pounds in my chest. "Oh gosh—really? I thought I still had time . . ."

"Doesn't matter. Just get outside." He hangs up before I can answer.

I rush into action, running upstairs, tugging on sneakers and a black hoodie, making sure to toss Billy some biscuits before I leave. On my way, I tenderly tuck my dad's picture into my backpack—for luck—before grabbing my flashlight and locking the door behind me.

Mike waits impatiently at the foot of my driveway, already straddling his bike. "What happened?" he hisses.

"Nothing—sorry," I say, picking up my bike and climbing on. "Let's just get this over with." I'm about to take off, when Mike grabs the side of my handlebar.

"Wait. I have something for you." From his pocket, he yanks out a gold bag of gummy bears. I smile, and as I take the packet, our fingers cling together.

"Thanks," I whisper, not wanting to let go.

"No problem, Parker."

We both pull up our hoods before flying into the night. We follow the same route that we took Sunday, but the Halloween decorations look much more sinister than they did in the daylight. There's a row of houses that have ghosts swinging from the trees on their front lawns, faces hand-drawn on pillowcases cinched around their would-be-necks. They sway ominously in the quiet breeze as Mike and I whoosh past, our legs moving faster with each block.

By the time we reach the cemetery, it's just shy of nine o'clock. We hide our bikes in the bushes, before dipping past the iron gate.

"Should we hide?" Mike asks.

I nod. "At least until we see Lex. I think the only thing we've got going for us right now is being able to surprise them."

We follow the winding gravel path around the gravestones, until we reach the large tree that drapes its leaves over the ground. Abigail's spot is frigid still. I can't help but notice how lonely it feels, like the sadness is in the air, settling over us.

Mike pulls me behind the oversized trunk, and we press our hands against the peeling birch as we wait for the Ladies in White to arrive.

In the distance, there's a rustling of leaves, and then I feel them, the cold from their ghostly forms causing me to shiver inside my hoodie. Mike follows my gaze across the cemetery.

The five ghosts move fluidly side by side, weaving around the graves, their eyes fixated on the tombstone in front of us. Lex walks with Abigail, their arms looped together. There's a dreamy expression on Lex's face, as if she's half-asleep. For a horrible second, I wonder if we're too late. But then I hear her voice, piercing the eerie silence.

"I never knew there was a restaurant through here," Lex says, looking around. "This sure is a weird shortcut."

The other Ladies in White ignore her, but Abigail gives

her a small smile and a pat on the arm. I want to launch forward and tear her claws away from my friend, but Mike grips my elbow, shaking his head.

I exhale into the tree and watch as they come to a halt in front of Abigail's grave.

Brea scowls at her surroundings. "I thought we were done with this."

Jade and Eleanor exchange worried looks. Eleanor whispers into Jade's ear, but for once they don't laugh or smile. Cami takes a large step closer to them, hugging herself against the wind.

Abigail holds up a hand to silence them, before turning her attention back toward Lex. "I have something special to share with you," she says, holding my friend's hands in her own. "Something that I've only ever shared with my daughters." She motions to Eleanor, Jade, Brea, and Cami.

Lex looks from the other Ladies in White, to Abigail, then back to the grave. "I don't understand . . ." She trails off, and I see a flash of fear in her eyes as she reads the inscription.

This is our chance. I nod once to Mike, before we both leap out from behind the tree.

"Stop!" I yell.

The Ladies in White spin around to look at us. An amused smile crosses over Abigail's lips.

"Well, well. Look who we have here," she purrs.

"Quinn?" Lex asks, gaping at me. "Mike? What are you guys doing here?"

"Saving you," I tell her, darting forward.

Abigail dodges me in one swift movement, and before I know it, I'm flanked on both sides by Eleanor and Jade. Brea glides around and locks Mike's arms in a death grip behind his back.

"What are you doing?" Lex cries. "Let them go!" She tries to step away, but Abigail won't let go of her hands. Lex's eyes widen. "Abigail?"

"It won't hurt at all, my dear," Abigail says, pulling her face close to Lex's. She flashes Mike and me an evil smile. "And now you'll have even more siblings, since your friends decided to interrupt our party."

A tear streams down Lex's cheek. "I—I want to go home."

Abigail gently swipes the tear away. "We will be home soon, dear. Very, very soon." She lifts a vial from the folds in her dress.

"No!" Cami cries. "You don't need to do this, Abigail."

"Cami, we've been *over* this," Abigail says, sighing as though she's losing patience with her youngest daughter.

"But Abigail, they *found* them."

At this, the vial slips through Abigail's fingertips and smashes to the ground, causing the poison to leak all over the dirt. Eleanor and Jade loosen their grip on my arms enough for me to twist away. I stumble forward, almost winding up in the gravel. Mike wrenches himself free from Brea and hurries to my side just as Abigail turns to us.

"Where?" she demands, her skin flickering like lightning. Her eyes go impossibly dark. "Where. Are. They?"

A billow of wind shoots across the space between us. Jade, Eleanor, Brea, and Cami exchange worried looks as their bodies turn translucent.

"We'll show you if you let go of Lex," I say, planting my feet onto the ground.

With one motion, Abigail shoves Lex toward us. Lex falls into my arms, her eyes filled with tears.

"Quinn, what's going on?" she pleads, but I don't answer. We don't have time.

"Let's show her, Quinn," Cami tells me, softening her voice. "It's the only way."

I point toward the Hudson house.

"Take me there," Abigail hisses.

I glance at Mike. He nods, and I lead the way across the street, not daring to let go of Lex.

The Ladies in White practically float across the driveway, following us around to the back, past the little pond, all the way to the three graves huddled together.

The pain in Abigail's face makes me almost feel sorry for her—almost, that is, until I remember that she's a ghost. A killer ghost who just tried to steal my friend's soul.

Still, it's hard to watch as she approaches the graves of her daughters. An inhuman cry escapes from the pit of her stomach, bringing her to her knees on the uneven earth. Her sobs ring out, and I recognize the sound of grief from my own father's funeral, when I had to lift my mom up from the dirt.

Cami, Brea, Eleanor, and Jade wrap their arms around Abigail as she rocks back and forth, hugging her knees to her chest. They all start to fade a bit.

Cami crouches forward to stroke back Abigail's hair, shushing her ghost mother as Abigail repeats the same phrase over and over again: "He took my babies—he took them ... He took my babies ..."

"What's going on?" Lex asks me. "I don't understand ..."

Mike and I exchange looks, but before I can even start to explain, the back door of the Hudson house swings open, and out steps Mrs. Hudson. Her silver hair is twisted into a braid, and her long, willowy body is draped in a colorful robe. Nurse Steph is nowhere in sight.

"It's Mrs. Hudson," Mike gasps.

She shuffles out of her home with her cane, her lips thinned in determination even though her body seems to protest each step.

"Abigail," she calls. Her voice is sharp and cuts through the air.

Suddenly, the crying stops, and all at once the graveyard

feels too quiet. Mike steps closer to me, and I step closer to Lex, our shoulders touching in a line.

"What do we do?" I whisper.

Mike just shakes his head, dumbstruck.

When Abigail finally stands, she seems to do it without any of her joints moving, almost like a puppet pulled up by strings. Her body appears larger, darker, more menacing. When she turns, her eyes are hollow and her mouth is fierce, pulled into a tight, thin line.

"Christopher moved the graves," Mrs. Hudson confesses, taking tiny steps forward. I can tell that she's trying to look brave, but I notice her hands shaking. "He just wanted peace for his girls." She nods toward the row of stones. "Let him rest. Let them all rest."

The lights inside the Hudson house start to flicker behind her. At first, it seems almost musical the way they twinkle on and off, as if following a silent beat. But when I steal a glance at Cami and see her worried expression, I know that something is wrong.

Suddenly, the lights stop flickering, and we're blanketed in darkness.

"What's happening?" Lex cries beside me, her voice coming out like a whimper. "I want to go—let's please just go . . ."

Mrs. Hudson digs inside the pocket of her robe, pulling out something gold and shiny—*two* gold and shiny somethings. Necklaces!

"These belonged to your girls," she explains. "I've kept them safe for you. I want you to have them. So that you can feel close to them again." She holds the chains out, letting them sparkle in the light of the moon.

Abigail's mouth stretches into an unnatural shape as she seems to exhale a gust of wind, sending the necklaces flying to the grass. "How. Dare. You!" she cries.

"It's OK," Jade says, trying her best to soothe Abigail. "Look—we've found them! It's what you've always wanted."

For a moment, everyone seems frozen, as if Abigail has somehow cast a spell across the grounds. And then the sound of metal scraping against concrete cuts through the eerie silence, followed by a loud bang and Mrs. Hudson's scream. The lights flash on just in time for us to watch a cast-iron patio table fly across the yard, smashing against the side of the house, just barely missing Mrs. Hudson's head.

I feel Lex slip down beside me, her body boneless and weak.

"She's fainted!" I cry to Mike. "Here, get her arm—"

"What do we do?"

"Just lay her down . . ."

"Should we run?"

"How?" I cry, pointing to Lex. "We can't move her like this."

As Mike and I scramble to keep Lex safe, furniture continues to fly around us as if we're caught in a cyclone. The crash of metal hitting wood makes a sound far worse than thunder, and I feel each *bang* in the pit of my chest even when I cover my ears with my hands.

"This isn't safe!" Mike cries. I can barely hear him over the noise.

My toes tingle, wanting nothing more than to run away as fast as I can. But we can't leave Lex. I dig my heels into the earth and brace myself against the windstorm swirling around us. The lights continue to flash until the yard looks like a strobe light. It's making me dizzy, and for a moment I'm afraid that I might throw up.

As if sensing my unsteadiness, Mike charges against the wind and pulls me toward him. We hold on to each other as we stand in front of Lex's unconscious body.

Mrs. Hudson, for her part, looks just as terrified as I feel, but she refuses to move.

"What are you doing?" I yell to her. "You need to *run!*"

Her eyes flicker to mine. "Didn't you tell me we have to help our friends, even if we're scared? Well, consider this helping. It's what I should have done a long time ago. I'm done running."

She digs her cane deeper into the lawn. "I'm sorry for your loss, Abigail," she cries out, her voice strained. "I'm sorry for everything. But you *must* let them go!"

A scream slices through the air as Abigail flails her arms above her head. Her features are unrecognizable now—distorted and inky black. Instead of flesh and bone, she seems to be made up of slashes and jagged lines. What's left of her human body stretches out above us until she's as tall as a tree. Her limbs sharpen like knives.

The other Ladies in White huddle together with fright in their eyes, as if they've never seen their ghost mother in this form—her truest form.

Abigail launches her arms forward, sending a metal shovel straight toward Mrs. Hudson's head.

I don't think. I just pull away from Mike and run toward her.

"Parker—wait!" Mike cries behind me.

"Stay with Lex!" I tell him. My legs guide me instead of my brain, and it isn't until I'm almost in front of the sharpest edge of the shovel that I start to wonder what I'm doing. I close my eyes and my dad's image pops into my mind. I start to whisper his name.

"Enough!"

The one word is powerful enough for me to open my eyes, and when I do, I see Cami standing in front of me, holding the shovel, facing Abigail.

"Step aside," Abigail hisses, her voice sounding no longer human.

"You will not hurt her," Cami says, stepping in front of me. "You will not hurt any of them."

As if on cue, the other Ladies in White take protective stances in front of Mrs. Hudson and me.

"Traitors—all of you!" Abigail snarls.

Hot tears fall down my cheeks. I can't tell whether it's relief, or fear, or both, but my chest hurts with every uneven breath that I take.

"It's over, Abigail," Cami continues, her tone softening. "Let them go."

"Never!"

"You need to let *all* of us go."

Abigail's features twist and turn, before her dagger-like fingers lash out and strike Cami from across the yard. Cami cries out as she's tossed back against the house. Brea goes to her as Eleanor and Jade stand off against Abigail.

"That wasn't right," Jade says, keeping her voice low and even. "Abigail, we're on your side."

"What do you know about sides?" Abigail hisses, sending a flash of lightning right toward Jade.

Eleanor reaches out and seems to catch the fire in her palm, launching it back at Abigail. Abigail takes the hit in what would be her chest. She growls again.

"Ingrates!" she bellows, calling the branches on the trees to shake. "Traitors!"

"You told us you were protecting us from the world," Cami tells her, getting back to her feet. "But we really needed protection against *you*!"

She rejoins her sisters, and the four of them form a line in front of Mrs. Hudson and me. They hold hands, and the energy emanating off them in waves is so strong that it makes Abigail scream. I'm about to take this chance to usher Mrs. Hudson inside when something glitters in the grass, catching my eye. *It's the necklaces!* Reaching forward, I carefully lift them up. Abigail spins toward me. I brace myself, expecting the worst, but suddenly something moves beyond the graves.

Three white orbs rise behind the stones as a warmth washes over us, seeming to melt my frozen tears. The orbs hover together—two small, one large—and as they circle around Abigail, her entire presence seems to shrink. Her limbs become less jagged, and her face becomes more and more human, until she's turned back into a woman.

"Christopher?" she whispers, her voice shaky and uncertain. "Emily? Ava?" She extends her hand as if to stroke the smallest orb, but it floats higher, just out of her reach. "My babies—my family . . ."

The Ladies in White relax their stance and follow their ghost mother to the edge of the yard, where the dark trees meet the stones. As if they were chasing fireflies, the five of them try to capture the lights with cupped hands as Mike runs over to me; our arms wrap tightly around each other. The orbs float higher and higher, their lights becoming so bright that I have to squint my eyes against the heat.

"No!" Abigail shrieks. "No—stay with me. Take me with you!" She swings her arms wildly, trying to catch any last sliver of light before they completely disappear.

Abigail's cries are enough to break her. Literally. All at once, the Ladies in White start to crack like porcelain dolls, the light bursting through the seams until the human forms disappear and all that remains is the whitest, hottest light.

Without thinking, I bolt forward, running across the grass until I'm standing in front of Cami. There's not much of her left, but I can still make out her face.

"Thank you," I whisper, holding out my hand.

Her face cracks as she smiles back, and I'm bathed in heat.

For a moment, I think that they're going to catch on fire, but instead they fade into nothing, and all that's left is darkness.

Mrs. Hudson collapses against the house, her hand clenched over her heart as she tries to slow her breathing. She looks at Mike, Lex, and me as if for the first time. "You must come inside, dears. We need to call someone to take you home."

I make my way back over to Mike, and we fall into each other's arms. I can feel his heart beating against mine, and we stay like this until Mrs. Hudson beckons us again.

"Coming," I tell her. I pull away from Mike. "I know who to call. You stay here with Lex."

He nods, and I start off toward the house. I realize that I'm still holding the girls' necklaces. Looking around, I don't see any sign of Abigail's. Could it have disappeared with the ghosts?

"Hurry, dear," Mrs. Hudson urges, holding open the door. I tuck the necklaces into my pocket, before following her into the old house that smells of cinnamon.

Grandma Jane shows up not even ten minutes later, with Red hustling at her side.

"Are you OK? What happened?" she asks, cupping my face in her hands. I breathe in the scents of banana bread and lavender.

"We're OK," I tell her, before falling into her arms.

I help Red and Mike carry Lex into the car as Grandma Jane goes inside to speak with Mrs. Hudson. When Grandma reemerges through the front door, she takes a bottle out of her oversized handbag and begins spritzing it all over the burial ground, gracefully throwing her hands around as if she were a dancer. She then makes her way back over to the car and finds the three of us huddled together in the backseat. Mike holds my hand as Lex lies against my shoulder. Without asking for an explanation, Grandma Jane and Red drive us home.

Just as we pull onto Main Street, Lex opens her eyes. "Where am I?" she asks, her voice groggy. "Did I fall asleep or something?"

"Seems so," Red says, saving Mike and me from answering.

She stretches her arms above her head. "I was having the most unbelievable dream. There were ghosts and flashing lights, and Abigail turned into this demon-thing . . ."

I hold my breath as Lex continues to talk a mile a minute about the events that she seems to have no memory of being real.

"It was so wild," she finally says, slumping back against the seat. She squints out of the window. "Hey, would you mind dropping me off at home? My mom's probably wondering where I am."

"Of course, honey."

We take a quick detour a few blocks over, and Mike and I help Lex to her door, despite her protests that she is capable of walking by herself. I can't help but notice that the color is already returning to her sunken cheeks, and I hug her fiercely before saying goodbye.

Grandma Jane steers us back to my house, eyeing me in the rearview mirror.

"Quinn Parker, that was stupid and dangerous."

I nod slowly. "I know, Grandma."

"Why didn't you come to us? We could have helped you, darling. Red and me."

"I just—we just . . . I thought we could handle it on our own," I finally say. "But you're right. It was stupid."

"You could have gotten your friend hurt."

"I know."

"You could have gotten killed!"

"I know."

She stares hard at me for a minute before easing into the faintest of smiles. "I'm just glad you're safe, sweetheart. My brave girl. You did handle it, didn't you? Like father like daughter."

Remembering, I dig into my backpack and pull out the photograph of my dad, hugging it to my chest for the rest of the ride home.

Once we get there, Grandma Jane fixes us all cups of steaming hot chocolate while Red lights a fire. I rest my head against Mike's shoulder as I allow the sweet drink to burn the tip of my tongue. My dad's photograph rests by my side, along with a sleeping Billy, and slowly, slowly, I feel myself begin to thaw.

CHAPTER 15

The sun shines over the cemetery, making it almost unrecognizable from the other night.

Mom holds my hand as we walk to Dad's grave. I can smell the scent of Grandma Jane's lavender oil as the breeze catches her hair.

"I'm glad you came with me today," she tells me, giving my hand a little squeeze.

"Me too," I say, and I mean it.

Who'd have thought that I'd cross these grounds four times in one month? I feel Dad everywhere, but especially here. Especially now.

"Do you want to sit?" Mom asks, motioning to the patch of grass in front of his gravestone.

Together, we kneel, resting a fresh batch of flowers by his name. Grandma Jane must have been here recently, because there's a new crystal in the dirt, too: this one is a smoky brown quartz that reminds me of Dad's eyes.

I think of those eyes staring back at me through the kitchen window. My heart doesn't seem to care anymore that it was Cami tricking me. I *felt* him with me that night. I feel him with me now.

Mom sniffles beside me, so I drop her hand and loop my arm around her shoulder. She wraps her arm around my waist. We stay this way, just remembering him. The unfunny jokes at dinner. The compliments he'd give Mom's cooking even when it was burnt to a crisp. The sound of his voice when he called me *kiddo*. His messy handwriting. The way he smiled with his whole body. His hugs. If I close my eyes, I can almost feel his arms around me. It brings me to tears.

"It's OK to cry," Mom asks, kissing the top of my hair.

And so I do, letting my mom hold me until my lungs feel full and my heart feels lighter. Then we help each other to our feet, wiping at our cheeks with the backs of our hands.

"You ready?" she asks.

"Can I just have one minute?"

She smiles. "Sure, honey. I'll go and start the car. Take your time."

I wait until she disappears past the gate.

"Bye, Dad," I whisper. "See you next time."

Then I trudge up the path, weaving in between the graves until I reach the big oak tree in the back corner. Slowly, I approach Abigail's grave.

"Hi, Abigail," I say. I pull the lockets out from my pocket, dangling them in front of me. "I thought you might want these." I place each one carefully on top of her stone; the gold catches the light through the tree—for once, making this spot look happy. A crow lands on the edge of one of the branches just as a cold breeze whips through my hair, giving me goosebumps.

"Goodbye, Abigail," I say, before darting back down the path.

EPILOGUE

"Do you have it on?" I whisper, pulling my head in close to Mike's.

He scowls at me. "I'm a man of my word, Parker. I'm not going to chicken out. It's under this." He gestures to his track suit, zipped up to the neck.

I grin and point to Lex and Zoe on the bleachers across the field, who wave their phones wildly in the air. "Good. My girls are armed and ready."

Mike shakes his head. "No! No pictures. That wasn't part of the deal."

"Well, you never said *no pictures* when we shook hands, which means that anything goes."

He frowns. "Coach is going to be so mad at me. I'm starting to wonder why I'm friends with you. You have a way of always getting me into trouble." But there's a glint in his eyes as he says it.

I nudge him in the arm. "You know you love it."

He smiles. "Maybe a little bit."

"Let's move, team. Huddle up!" Coach yells across the field.

"It's go time," I tell Mike.

He shakes his head. "I can't believe I'm going to do this."

"Don't forget, it was *your* idea."

"Yeah, but I wasn't supposed to lose!"

"Well, maybe next time you won't doubt my instincts, Science Boy."

Mike takes off his Yankees hat and flings it across the sidelines. "Whatever, Parker. Let's just get this over with."

We warm up with the rest of the team, until Coach divides us up by event. Mike is up first. I can't keep a straight face as he approaches the line, still wearing his zippered track suit.

"Warren! Where's your uniform?" Coach calls.

"Right here, sir." Mike slowly unzips his suit, leaving him standing in a bright green, spandex Robin costume, complete with billowing cape.

Coach's eyes widen. "What the?"

"I lost a bet, Coach," Mike admits, flexing into his best superhero pose as both teams behind him wail with laughter.

"Nah, no way—nope!" Coach cries, shaking his head furiously. "Not having it. Ken, can we get an extra five minutes for my kid to change?"

The coach from the other team is practically bent over laughing. "Aww, come on, Mitch! Let the kid take a lap. A bet's a bet, right?"

Coach's face turns so red that, for a moment, I think he might burst. He holds up one finger and points to Mike. "One. Lap. Then you get your head on straight, you hear me? This is a track meet, not a circus."

"Got it, Coach!"

Mike snaps on a small black eye mask before taking his mark, his cape flying out behind him. I cheer from the sidelines, and Mike throws me a wink. When the gun goes off, he bolts into action, a flash of green, taking off like the bullet he is. The crowd goes wild, and it takes everything in Coach's power to try and keep the team focused. Even Jess is giggling.

"Hey, Quinnie!" Zoe and Lex wave me down by the fence.

I trot over and hover near them, just out of Coach's line of sight. Lex is looking just like her old self again. Today, she's rocking a black shirt with purple jeans and red sneakers. Her skin is flushed and very much alive.

"I figured out our group Halloween costume," she tells me.

"Really? What?" I ask.

"Your old neighbors! Wouldn't that be amazing? But I call dibs on Ms. Bea. She was definitely the most glam."

I feel my mouth drop open, speechless.

"Hello? Quinnie? You still there?"

Luckily, Zoe changes the subject before I can cough out an answer. "Look! Your boy is about to cross the finish line!" She aims her camera on him, before pushing me forward. "Go get him!"

"Yeah," Lex says, "we'll find you later!"

I spin around just as Mike takes his final strides, pumping his fists into the air and hamming it up for the crowd. Everyone loves it except for Coach.

"You get your cape into that locker room and don't come back until you're decent!" he yells.

"Yes, Coach."

Mike saunters over to me, his hands on his hips as he catches his breath. He lifts the mask to the top of his head.

"Nice job, Robin," I tell him with a smile.

"Thanks, Batman."

He holds out his hand for me to take, his cape surging out behind us. Our shadows stretch across the turf, making us look large and invincible, like two kids who can take on the world and all of the monsters in it.

Bring it on, South Haven.

We squeeze our palms together, until Mike finally pulls away.

"Guess I should change," he tells me.

"Guess so."

I watch him make his way toward the field house, my fingers still buzzing even as I stand alone. The sun warms me from within, and I stretch my face up toward it, soaking in its light.

"Quinn!" Coach yells from the sidelines. "What the heck are you doing over there? Sunbathing? Come on!"

The sound rushes back to my ears, jolting me awake, sending an energy down my spine and to my calves, waking them up. I take the deepest of breaths, bracing my muscles and my bones to do what I do best.

I fly.

ACKNOWLEDGMENTS

It was an honor to write another Fright Watch book, and I am full of gratitude to all the folks at Abrams Kids for giving me this opportunity. Thank you to Amy Vreeland, Jade Rector, Jenn Jimenez, Patricia McNamara O'Neill, Jenny Choy, Megan Evans, Hallie Patterson, Maggie Lehrman, Jody Mosley, Andrew Smith, Richard Slovak, Gilles Ketting, and David Coulson. And special thanks to my amazing editor, Emily Daluga. Not only have you championed this series, but your notes are always spot on, and your monster knowledge is unmatched! I have become a better storyteller because of you, and this makes me feel so lucky.

Of course, huge thanks are owed to my friends and family, especially my mom, my husband, and my kids. You give me time, encouragement, laughter, hugs, and tea. Lots and lots of tea . . . I'd also like to thank my agents, past and present: Amy Tipton and Kathleen Rushall.

But most of all, I'd like to thank YOU, dear reader. Thank you for joining Quinn and Mike on another adventure. I hope you enjoyed your time on Goodie Lane.

ABOUT THE AUTHOR

Lorien Lawrence is a writer and middle school English teacher from Connecticut. When she's not buried under a stack of books, she can be found exploring spooky haunts with her family.